MW01405106

GUARDED BY A MONSTER

KENZIE KELLY

Website & Newsletter: http://www.kenziekelly.com
Instagram: @exlibiriskenzie

Cover illustration by Nyx.

Typography and formatting by Kenzie Kelly.

Chapter header illustrations by Kit Fox.

Editing by Dayna Hart.

kenzie kelly

For everyone who thought Drym and Kendal went from zero to naked—buckle up, buttercups.

Getting Jade and Thurl to bang was like trying to roast marshmallows with a single flickering match in the middle of a hurricane.

ONE

I'D LOST MY glasses more times than Velma and I wished like hell this was one of those times. I did not want to see what I was witnessing. Not only was I unable to tear my eyeballs away but the glasses I'd cursed since I was 6 years old made everything stand out in ultra-high definition.

I was a kindergarten teacher, for Christ's sake. I should never have been a murder witness, but there I was, in a downtown Damruck alley trying to tempt a cute little tuxedo cat out from under a dumpster with seafood medley paté while a man at the far end stabbed somebody.

My knees were screaming in protest at the awkward crouch I'd held for far too long but I didn't dare move. The late summer air hung thick and heavy in the alley, making the metallic scent of blood somehow worse. It wasn't late enough for the shadows to turn deep and any move I made had the potential to draw the eyes of more than the stray cat. If I thought I'd get away with it, I'd have crawled under the dumpster with them. I chanced a glance at the ground and decided that no, I actually wouldn't. Behind a Chinese restaurant was a great place for stray cats, but the ground was five miles from anything clean. I'd never be able to squeeze my big ass under there anyway.

The blood streaming down the victim's chest was almost purple. It didn't look like that in the movies, but that was a ridiculous thought to be having right then. The whole scene was a lot quieter, too. I think the victim grunted once or twice, but the whoosh of blood in my ears was better than any noise-canceling headphones.

My thighs shook. I was certain I was going down in a heap, but then it was over. Without the blood and the odd flash of metal from the blade, I would've thought the murderer was just punching the other man. Once, twice, maybe four times was all it took and then the victim crumpled to the asphalt and his assailant hightailed it into the night.

I knew better than to try to stand, so I just fell on my butt. The stray cat and I shared a look before it took off like its tail was on fire. The adrenaline coursing through me wanted to follow it. My shirt clung to my back in the humid air, and somewhere a fan rattled against ancient brick. I was torn about what to do. I needed to check for a pulse, but the amount of blood and lack of even an eye twitch made me think it was futile. And if I did that, I risked contaminating evidence. I'd watched enough Investigation Discovery not to go tramping through a crime scene.

It took the phone in my pocket blooping for me to remember it existed. I leaned to the side and reluctantly put my hand down to balance so my other one could fish the cell out of my back pocket. I dropped it twice before I finally managed to get it unlocked and dial.

"Nine-one-one. What is the nature of your emergency?"

"Um… I just witnessed a murder. Maybe."

"You *maybe* witnessed a murder?"

"I definitely witnessed something. I just can't be one hundred percent certain that the victim is dead."

"Have you checked their pulse?"

"I considered it."

"But you haven't done it? Is the assailant still present?"

"No, and no. I didn't want to mess up the crime scene."

"Ma'am, I'm going to need you to check for a pulse."

"Okay." I grunted and groaned my way through getting to my feet. Then dropped my phone again. "Damn it, sorry, I'm shaking like I've got palsy and I dropped my phone again."

"That's okay, Ma'am. Have you checked for a pulse?"

"I'm walking to the body." My knees screamed when I crouched next to the head. I gasped. He couldn't have been out of high school.

"Are you okay?"

"I'm fine, it's just… he's so young." My index and middle finger sank into the side of his neck and I rooted around for a bit. "I can't find a pulse."

"What is your location?"

"I'm in the alley behind Chow Man's Land."

"I have police and EMS on the way. I need you to stay there and on the line with me until they arrive. What is your name?"

"Jade Massey. Can I go inside? I'm kind of hungry."

The pause from the other end of the phone was long enough to be awkward. "I haven't eaten since breakfast. I'm a kindergarten teacher, and one of my students is having a rough time at home, so I've been giving her my lunch to let her skip the cafeteria. Then as I was heading home, Emma from Dixie Whiskers called and asked me to come here and try to catch a tuxedo that's been hanging around. It's probably not appropriate to be hungry after witnessing a murder, but I watch a lot of crime shows so I guess it hasn't hit me the way it might someone else?"

"Ma'am?"

"And Chow Man's Land is the best Asian food in Damruck. If you haven't been you gotta try the dim sum Sunday buffet, and the dinner rush must be happening because there's all sorts of yummy smells coming from their back door."

"Jade!"

"Sorry. I talk too much when I'm nervous."

"That's all right."

The operator switched her voice to patient grandmother mode and even though I registered what she was doing; it calmed me down. I inhaled until my lungs burned and then slowly let the air out. "I hear sirens!" I kept my happy dance restrained.

"Yes ma'am. Tell me when the first to arrive is on scene."

"A police officer has just parked at the far end of the alley."

"I'll let them take it from here, then."

I hadn't even finished my, "Okay, bye," before I heard the click. I went to rub my eyes and then remembered that hand was on the ground. Water dripped steadily from a rusty air conditioning unit above, making me jump at each plunk against the metal dumpster.

I needed to wash my hands. I was probably immune to everything but Ebola, but I still didn't slack on personal disease prevention. Working with twenty of the world's best disease vectors for a few years will do that to you.

The police officer exited her patrol car and I waved at her like I was inviting her into the backyard picnic.

"Jade Massey?"

I nodded.

"Are you okay?"

"Yep." I pressed my lips together to keep the stream of words from flowing.

"Please walk to me, keeping as close to the building as possible."

I did as I was told, trying to appear as normal as possible. When I got close enough, she stuck out her hand. My capacity to make things weird knows no bounds, apparently. "You don't want to touch me. I had to sit on the ground next to the dumpster. I mean, I had to put my hand on the ground to dig my phone out of my pocket." I looked around like a sink and soap would appear in the alley.

The striking woman stared at me the way I looked at the first kid I caught picking boogers each year. She dropped her hand to her side and took a step back. "Right. Do you have blood on your skin or clothing?"

I shook my head. "I was pretty far away. I don't think the killer ever saw me."

"Let's hope not."

The murmur of her voice continued under my head exploding. "Am I in danger?"

After her pointed look, I peeled my fingers away from her bicep and took a step back.

"A detective will determine your level of risk after taking your statement."

I nodded and picked at the skin next to my thumbnail. "Can I wait inside? I'm hungry and want to wash my hands."

A flock of police cars trailed a silent ambulance that wedged itself into the narrow opening of the alley. The police officer I'd grabbed with my grubby hand closed her eyes and pinched the bridge of her nose. "I'll escort you to the restroom."

The *but I don't wanna* was as loud as if she'd actually said it.

TWO

I ROLLED OVER for the hundredth time. No matter what I tried, I couldn't get comfortable. The bed was too soft, the house too quiet. I should be thankful for both. It wasn't long ago my brothers and I were trapped in a lab, continually poked and prodded by scientists and subject to their every whim.

Some of my brothers had adapted to freedom well. Not me. I was on constant alert, waiting for the spotlights, the shouting of soldiers, the pounding of boots signaling our capture.

I wanted to relax. I wanted to enjoy the freedom we'd won with our fangs and claws, but I couldn't quite manage it. I gave up and got out of bed. I wandered down the hall into my kitchen. Our specially designed houses had tall ceilings and industrial strength appliances—a far cry from the small, sterile confines of the lab.

My ears flicked, searching for any sound out of place. There were none. I stepped outside into the night and took a deep breath. No unusual smells. Fireflies flicked in the shelter of the trees making lazy loops.

I made a concerted effort to lower my shoulders and stretch my fingers out of their usual fists.

My brothers and I were created for a specific reason, and each of us filled a role within our team of six. Roul and I were the muscle. We protected the others. Identified threats first, and were the first to go in on any mission.

Kendal, Drym's mate, said it was natural for us to still be on edge. We'd been free less than a year. She also declared us touch starved and hugged each of us every day. I looked forward to those hugs more than I cared to admit.

My ears twitched as a faint sound carried through the woods. Without thinking, I moved forward. Our preserve was large, but a neighborhood backed up to it on one side. The home site I'd chosen was closest to it. I knew better than to wander this close to humans, but I was bored and it was the middle of the night.

I reached the fence that encircled our property and scaled it easily, landing softly on the other side. The trees were thinner here, so I stayed as far in the shadows as I could manage.

The source of the sound stood on a small stoop, outlined by light spilling from an open door. Her hair shone like the sun as it flowed around her shoulders and down her back. She took a hesitant step onto the grass, then another that brought her closer. I willed her to keep going, to enter the forest and wrap her arms around me.

An impossible dream. I was a monster. She would run screaming if she saw me.

She stood so close I could smell her fear. Anger rose in my chest, swift and complete. I scanned the area for any threat but found none.

"Where is that furball?" She crouched down and whisper yelled, "Kitty, kitty! Dinner!" She tapped the side of a metal bowl. "Whisker McFluff, come on up."

Behind her, several cats watched her with varying levels of interest. Most seemed focused on the bowl she held, rather than her. One rubbed against her leg and meowed loud enough to make me twitch.

All the feline heads swiveled toward me.

The woman stood and seemed to stare directly at me. I held my breath and locked my muscles. After a few moments, she sighed, put the bowl down, and went inside, herding the cats away from the door as it closed.

I watched as she wandered through her house until she disappeared and all the lights went off. I crept closer, sniffing at the bowl of cat food she'd left out for the wayward feline and chasing a fresh, light scent from where she stood to the doorknob.

Under the fear, she smelled like sugar and sunshine.

Was she afraid for her missing cat, or was she scared of something else?

I went back to the meager shadows of the tree line and settled into a crouch. I decided since I was already awake, I would watch over her. I wouldn't let anything hurt her, and she could rest.

An hour later, I heard almost imperceptible footfalls stalk closer. I tilted my head at the gray-and-white striped cat that sat next to me.

"Are you Whisker McFluff?"

"Merreow."

"You shouldn't scare your mistress like that."

The cat purred and rubbed against my leg. I drew my silicone-coated claw down its back and marveled at the feel of its fur under my hand. So many new things we'd been able to experience since escaping the lab. Thanks to Kendal, we no longer had to fear our claws accidentally slashing something. She kept a steady supply of what she called “wyrfang claw caps” available. The silicone caps fit snugly over our claws, dulling them enough to lessen our worry. We still had to be careful, but we could touch things without slicing them to ribbons.

Mine were purple.

“Come on then,” I said to the cat, “let’s see if we can get you inside where you belong.”

I crept toward the back door, making sure the cat followed. I grumbled at finding it unlocked. Silly female. It had to be the cat she feared for—otherwise she would have locked her door, right? In either case, I would continue to watch over her.

Her smell was stronger with the door open. I took a deep breath, trying to memorize every nuance of the scent. Standing in the doorway, the cat purring as it rubbed figure eights around my legs, I felt a sense of peace.

“Who’s there?” Her voice was soft but steady, like someone used to calming frightened creatures.

I leaped back, crouching to make myself as small as possible as I scurried to the relative safety of the tree line. I pricked my ears and turned my head to train my good eye on her, adjusting my stance to compensate for the permanent reminder of the lab's cruel tests.

My jaw clenched. *We should put him down and start over. He is damaged and may not be useful anymore.*

I shook off the memory and trained my focus on the woman.

"Oh!" She scooped the cat into her arms. "Whisker!" I heard her sniffle. "You stay inside, you bad kitty." She put the wayward feline indoors, then stepped onto the small stoop and closed the door behind her. One step forward, and she reached the end of the small block of concrete.

She wrapped her arms around her torso, and my own itched to pull her against me. She squinted and took a deep, shaky breath.

"Thank you for bringing him back to me. You'll never know how much I needed all of my friends tonight."

She stepped back inside and moved around her kitchen. She came back out moments later with two small bowls and set them on the edge of the patio.

"Food and water for you. Maybe in time you'll be less shy."

She locked the door behind her this time and I relaxed. I listened to the mumble of her voice as she berated Whisker for being naughty until even that disappeared into the darkness inside her house.

She thought I was a stray cat. Or maybe a dog. Warmth radiated from my chest until it filled my entire body. She wanted to care for me. I'd be damned if I let her efforts go to waste. I drained the water and scooped the cat food into my palm. I'd leave it for the family of raccoons who lived in the woods.

As the first streaks of dawn lit the sky, I made my way back to my house and slept nightmare-free for the first time in a long while.

THREE

A DOOR SLAMMED somewhere down the hall and Sophia jumped. This was the best and worst part of my job. She was a cute little girl with brown ringlets and enormous eyes that skittered around the room.

"It's okay, just another class going to lunch."

She stared at me for a few long moments, then took another bite of her sandwich.

When I met her at the beginning of the school year, I knew something was off. I'd had shy students before, but Sophia cowered in the corner and always kept her back to the wall. She immediately took me up on my offer of eating lunch in the classroom, but it was a month and a half before she said a single word.

I couldn't point to visible bruises, malnutrition or any other obvious signs of abuse, but the little girl's behavior was enough for me. The way she flinched at sudden movements and wore long sleeves even in warm weather told its own story. I wanted to contact the authorities immediately, but administration said there wasn't enough evidence. Every day at lunch I chatted with her. They were one-sided conversations, but I hoped she would open up before long.

The school's resource officer poked his head in, jerking his chin toward Sophia in question. I shook my head and he left, a frown furrowing his brows. Oscar was a kind, older man who worked as a detective for years before transferring to the school. Probably in his fifties, with salt and pepper in his short cropped coils, but he kept his body fit. I could tell he'd seen things no one should ever witness. He agreed with me about Sophia. Something at home wasn't right. We watched over her, helped her feel safe in every way we could, but until she opened up, neither one of us could do more to help.

He'd met me in the parking lot that morning.

"Heard you had quite the ordeal last night. Y'alright?"

"I'm okay. Shaken a bit, but the officers assured me there's no reason the perpetrator would come after me. They want me to come to the station and work on a composite."

He nodded. "I doubt he saw you. Would'a been too focused on his task." He shook his head. "Drug deal gone wrong, most like."

Neither man had looked like an addict, but the only thing I knew about that was from movies and TV, and that was clearly unreliable. "That's what they said."

"Keep your windows and doors locked and you'll be fine." He chuckled. "Those cats of yours would probably scratch his eyes out if he tried messin' with you."

I smiled at the thought. Most of my rescues were former ferals who ran and hid when they heard anything unfamiliar. I doubt I could rely on them for protection.

I thought about the strange animal that watched from the treeline. At first I assumed it was another cat that Whiskers was carousing the neighborhood with. Then I saw the red reflection from its eyes and realized it was much larger than a cat. Maybe a big dog.

I can see enough without my glasses to putter around my house, and after witnessing the murder, I left them off for the rest of the night. I did wish I'd grabbed them to get a better look at what brought Whiskers home. The food and water I put out were gone that morning, so I decided to put more out for it when I got home.

Sophia was staring at me when I refocused, so I launched back into the story I was telling her about looking for Whiskers. "He's doesn't usually try to get out, so I was scared he wouldn't find his way home. Lucky for me, he found a friend who showed him the way."

"A friend?"

Her voice was so low I almost couldn't hear her. I nodded. "I'm not sure who the friend was. I thought another cat maybe, but it seemed too big for another cat. Maybe a dog. Whatever it was, I'm just glad it brought Whiskers back to me."

The bell signaled the end of lunch and she hadn't spoken again, but I counted that day as a victory. She'd said something! Out loud! Like taming a feral cat, progress was measured in minute degrees.

I made it through the rest of the afternoon with half a brain. The other half focused on thoughts of Sophia, the murderer, and the mysterious critter in my backyard. By the time I'd finished for the day, I was exhausted. I slumped into the seat of my RAV4 and let my head fall back.

Startled awake by tapping on my window, I put my hand over my heart and yelled, "Jesus, Oscar, you gave me a heart attack!"

"Sorry. I didn't mean to scare you. Just wanted to make sure you're okay. I'm heading out."

I turned the car battery on and rolled down the window. "I'm okay. Just tired."

"You've had a long day. Want me to follow you home?"

I smiled. "No, thank you, I'll be okay."

He hesitated, his lips pressed into a line. After a long moment, he nodded. "Okay then. Drive safe."

"I will."

Before he thought better of letting me go without an escort, I cranked the engine and pulled out. I didn't live far, but I went past the turn for my house and into a drive through. I was sure the cats would flay me for being late with their dinner, but I needed to eat, too.

I pulled into my driveway with half of my fries and drink gone. I gathered my things, locked the car, and made my way to the door with keys in hand. My huge orange tabby, Sir Purrs-a-lot, stared at me from the living room window. As I slipped my key into the lock, he wailed like he was starving.

"I know, I know. I'm coming. You aren't going to starve because your dinner is two hours late."

I waded through a mass of swirling bodies, lashing tails and plaintive meows. My hands shook slightly as I reached for the cabinet - they hadn't really stopped since last night, but I'd gotten better at hiding it. I set what was left of my dinner beside the sink and got to work picking up empty dishes and pulling various medicines and food out of the cabinet dedicated to cats.

By the time I had everything ready and placed bowls back into their places on the kitchen floor, everyone had lined up and most waited patiently. The kitten I'd added recently sang the song of her people loudly to make sure I wouldn't forget to feed her. After making sure everyone was at the right bowl, I moved to the sink. My hands dripped soap into the sink with small plops, the running water forgotten as a glowing red eye stared at me from the backyard.

It had to be Whiskers' friend. Maybe a bobcat? It was too far off the ground, though. Bobcat in a tree? I stared at it while my mind puzzled out what I was looking at. My hands itched and I realized I'd been staring so long the soap was drying. I rinsed quickly and grabbed a spare bowl and a can of food.

I sat on the back step while I opened the can. If the sound didn't lure them closer, the smell of stinky tuna would. Staying low, I set the bowl halfway between my door and the tree line and sat on the stoop.

"Come on, it's okay." I spoke softly with a higher tone. Something told me I'd need to pull out all my taming tricks for this one—if it even could be tamed. "I'm not going to hurt you, I promise. Come eat. I'll stay right here."

I got a slow blink for my trouble. The rustle of leaves marked its slow descent to the ground, but the eye reflection was still impossibly high, even for a Maine Coon or Norwegian Forest Cat. Too big even for a bobcat. Could it be a panther?

I stuffed a laugh so I didn't scare it. I remembered my uncle's story of seeing a panther in the woods. Only in his southern accent it was p-aa-n-tha. He swore he'd seen it with his own two eyes, but there'd never been a confirmed sighting in Tayki county. Or any of the adjacent counties, for that matter.

Only one eye reflected. Had it lost the other? Poor thing. I couldn't make out any other details. It never came closer, and the night was too dark, my porch light too dim.

Eventually, I saw the eye disappear, as if the animal turned. The crackle of leaves and snapped twigs marked its departure.

I sighed. "Okay, I'll try again tomorrow."

My knees creaked and a grunt helped me stand. I sighed again and retreated to my cold hamburger and watered down drink.

FOUR

I COULDN'T STAY away. It was wrong and probably creepy for me to stand just out of sight in her backyard and watch her.

She'd come home late and seemed exhausted. What worries did she carry that were weighing her down? Not that I could help her. I would terrify her if I answered her call and came into the light. She would scream and run.

Even if, by some miracle, she didn't, I was broken. Unworthy of someone so perfect.

I tried to talk myself out of going. I even turned around twice. I just couldn't force my paws to move toward my house.

I told myself that maybe if I saw her again, it would release this tether. This pull toward her I couldn't seem to overcome.

I had no idea why I felt so possessive of her, wanted to protect her with everything I had. I'd only seen her once.

But she cared for me.

No. Not me.

The animal she thought I was.

That didn't matter. I had a primal need to ensure she was safe. I would just check on her, make sure she was okay and not missing any other cats.

But when I got there, she wasn't home. I waited, my eyes trained on her house, until I finally heard her car pull into the drive. I watched as she fed her cats first.

Then she stepped outside.

The scent of warm sugar flooded my nose and I closed my eyes to breathe deep. The sharp sound of metal being ripped heralded the smell I craved being obliterated by something awful. I put my hand over my nose to try to block it out.

Her soft voice made me still. She was looking right at me. I almost panicked, wondering how she could see me. She wasn't looking at me, but my eye. My one good eye still glowed red in the dark.

I shifted and eased onto my haunches. She expected a small animal, so I tried to look like one. I kept still until she stopped talking. She wrapped her arms around her middle and I wondered if she was cold.

She wasn't going back inside. She wouldn't as long as I was still there.

I turned and shuffled away, making as much noise as possible. I heard her deep sigh. Her door opened and closed. And I went back, staying close to a tree in case I needed to use it to shield my eye from view. I needn't have worried. She never looked toward the trees again.

I waited until the last light clicked off. Ten minutes later, I snuck close to the house, pausing below each window to listen. The one to the far right side was cracked open, and warm sugar once again filled my nose. I could hear her breathing, deep and slow and even.

I took a risk and stood up, wanting to see her one more time. The blinds were closed. Disappointed, I trudged to the back step and considered the stinky glop in the bowl she'd left for me. The raccoons would love it, but I'd have to carry it in my hand. I shuddered, gagged, and quickly dumped it into my palm. I stuck my hand out as far from my body as I could and stuck my nose in the crook of my other elbow.

The raccoons were waiting when I got to their tree. They chittered as I set down the foul-smelling chunks. "Don't get used to this. I may not go back, or she might tire of feeding me."

The littlest one patted my leg with its paw before it grabbed a sizeable chunk and scurried away.

I ran the rest of the way home and didn't bother closing the door before shoving my hand under the tap and scrubbing with the flowery soap Kendal bought for me. Even after washing three times, my palm still smelled awful. I made a mental note to ask Kendal what it was and how to get rid of the odor.

A tiny scrape against the wood floor spun me around. I dropped into a ready crouch and flexed my claws.

"Relax. It's just me." Quin stepped out of the shadows and into the small circle of my kitchen light.

My eyes narrowed. "What are you doing here at this time of night?"

"Where were you?"

"Out for a walk."

He hummed. "Can't sleep?"

I shook my head. "It's too quiet."

Nodding, he said, "Yeah. I can't either." He laughed. "Isn't that funny? We couldn't wait to leave the lab and all its beeping machines and scientists poking us at all hours and now here we are,"—he spread his hands wide—"free and unable to sleep because it's too quiet."

"Kendal says we'll adjust."

His hand scrubbed from his forehead to his nose before dropping off. He stared at the ceiling. "Yeah."

I wanted to be alone, but I wouldn't turn my brother away. "Do you want to stay?"

I expected him to make a joke. Some smart quip that would make me laugh and mask whatever he was feeling.

Instead, he simply looked at me and nodded. We piled together into my bed and slept. He was gone when I woke up the next morning.

That night, we repeated our actions. I stayed with the woman until she was asleep, then took food that was meant for me to the raccoons.

Quin would join me an hour or two later.

After a week, it was a solid nightly habit. Until the night everything changed.

FIVE

IT HAD BEEN another long day. Sophia still wouldn't talk to me, I wasn't any closer to seeing the animal in my backyard, and I was on edge waiting for a detective to call me about the murder.

All I wanted was to get home and soak in a hot tub until my fingers and toes went all pruney.

I dragged myself from the car, pulling my bag over my shoulder. I was digging out my keys when a loud meow chastised me for being late the third time this week. "Okay, hold your britches, Sir, I'm coming."

The big orange tabby shook his head as if to say it wasn't fast enough and meowed again.

The meow turned into a hiss. I looked at the window to find him with his back bowed, staring at something behind me. I spun. A small mouth set into an angular face bit out, "Bitch!" Pain exploded through my temple. As I fell, something huge streaked across the yard taking the man with it.

I rolled over and struggled to keep my head where it belonged. It felt like I'd lost it and it was rolling away. I needed to catch it, but how could I, without eyes to see where it went? A searing pain streaked through my brain. Must still be attached, then. I made it onto my hands and knees and spread both to stop the wobbling.

Sir Purrs-a-lot growled from the window as a fight raged behind me. I paid both no mind. My hands made it onto the first step and I told myself to breathe. Hands on the second step, I moved my half-ton knee onto the first. I struggled to rebalance and fell onto my side with a grunt.

My head swam and I contemplated the pros and cons of just staying there.

Pro: I would no longer have to move and the world might stop spinning too fast. I could lay there and take a nap.

Con: my assailant and a dark mass rolled across the grass. Or maybe the grass was rolling underneath them? I couldn't be sure, but in any case, they were still there.

I tilted my head back and stared at my front door. It was only a few feet, but it may as well have been a mile. When had I gained so much weight? I didn't remember my bones being made of lead. I should get inside and dial 911, but the distance seemed impossible.

A grunt turned scream ended abruptly and I closed my eyes. I'd just rest here for a minute. Then I'd go inside.

Why did I need to go inside? The steps were perfectly comfortable.

A rough voice scraped over my skin, goosebumps rising in its wake. "Are you okay?"

I dragged my eyelids up but couldn't see anything but a dark blur. My glasses must have been knocked off. I went to shake my head and winced. "I don't think so. My head…" I thought I'd raised my hand to wave at the side of my head, but when I looked again, my fingers just twitched where they lay on the step.

"Don't move. I'm calling for help."

"Can't move lead bones, anyway."

"Cavi, I need you. A woman was struck in the head."

I was almost asleep when his voice sent shivers over me again.

"I don't know! Just get here! And bring Kendal."

I winced at his tone. He was furious with whoever he was talking to.

"I'm sorry, little one. I'm not angry, just frustrated. Cavi should know I can't answer questions about your condition. I wouldn't have called him if I knew what to do."

I didn't realize I'd said that out loud. "S'okay." Ice flowed from my head to my toes. "When'd it get so cold?"

A growl, so low and inhuman it stood every hair on end, sounded from the end of the walk. Warmth suffused my back, and despite being draped over concrete steps and my head alternating between ten thousand degrees and negative forty, I relaxed. I felt protected, even though I was dimly aware I should feel anything but. The shadowy form above me shifted, and even through my blurred vision, I could tell he was built like a linebacker. But his touch, when he checked my head, was impossibly gentle. A deep sigh left my body and I sank into the feeling of safety.

SIX

I LAY STILL, not wanting to jostle her. Cavi had said to keep her still until he could assess her. The phone tucked into my hoodie vibrated, and I moved as little as possible, tilting my head so my good eye could see the text. Everyone was on their way.

I winced.

Everyone meant my five brothers and Kendal. They'd want answers about why I was anywhere near the human neighborhood. Why I'd killed the piece of shit on her lawn. I sighed and she snuggled back into me. I wanted to throw my arms around her and hold her tight. I wanted to take her back to my house and never let her out of my sight again.

It was an impossible dream.

The wyrfang's van pulled in behind her car and my brothers poured out of the side door. Cavi came directly to me while the others fanned out around the yard. None of us needed to be told what to do. Tactical maneuvers were what we were literally made for.

I growled as Cavi's hands probed her head and neck, her arms and legs. "She wasn't hit on her arms or legs, Cavi." The venom in my tone shocked me.

His eyes popped to mine. "All right. She took a good hit on the head and maybe has a concussion. A human doctor should see her."

"Fuck. I wish I could kill him again."

"We'll let you tear him apart after we get her taken care of." He turned to Kendal, standing nearby, her face a mask of worry. "We need your help."

"Anything."

My heart warmed. We'd been shown kindness only once before Kendal—when we escaped our captors. Our creators. Her daily hugs reminded us that not all touch hurt. She was kind and gentle and each of us would give our lives for hers.

He turned back to me. "You'll need to carry her to the van. Gently. Try not to jostle her too much."

I nodded and scooped her into my arms, ignoring the way she felt like she belonged there. I set her down in the back and fought the urge to crawl in with her. Kendal would take her to the hospital. Somewhere I couldn't go.

She laid a small hand on my forearm. "I'll take good care of her, Thurl." She pointed over my shoulder. "Help your brothers clean up. I'll keep you updated with text messages and call when I can."

I felt empty when I pulled my arms from around her. "Thank you."

Kendal nodded. I watched as she slowly backed the van out of the driveway and disappeared down the street.

I turned around to face the gauntlet of my brothers.

"What the actual fuck, Thurl?" Quin, ever forthright, said.

Kragen put a hand on Quin's shoulder. "Let's not interrogate him, Quin. Let him explain."

Our leader was a strategist. A tactical mastermind. Like any older brother, he was harsh when needed, but we knew he loved us.

"I went for a walk in the woods last week. I couldn't sleep. I ended up here." I shrugged.

I knew they wouldn't let it go at that, but it was worth a try.

“And then what?”

I looked up at him. “And then I saw her. In the backyard, calling for a cat. She was worried, so when the cat appeared a minute later, I put him inside.”

After a moment of dead silence, Quin snorted. “I’d get more information from a rock. Even Roul talks more than you.”

“I talk.” Roul grumbled from the edge of the group.

Quin waved a hand as if to say *see?*

Kragen rubbed the bridge of his muzzle. “Go on, Thurl.”

“I came back the next night to check on her.” I hung my head. “And every night since. Tonight, she wasn’t home when I arrived, so I waited. I was only going to stay until she got safely inside, but then that,”—I pointed to the dead man—“came out of the bushes, snarled at her and then hit her on the side of the head with something. She slumped to the ground and I…”

Kragen dipped his head to look into my eyes.

I stared at the ground, not wanting to answer.

“You what, Thurl?”

“I lost it. I tore him away from her, and he was dead before I really knew what I was doing.”

Cavi stood from where he’d crouched next to the body. “He ripped him apart.”

I looked at my hands, covered in blood. My claw caps were gone. Probably torn to shreds inside the body.

Kragen sighed. "Let's get this cleaned up and go home."

The flash as Drym took a photo on his phone momentarily blinded all of us. He shrugged in apology. "We should see if Bacon or Bull can find out who he is. That'll help determine if she was targeted or just a random victim."

The idea that someone could target her, that someone would plan violence against her, made my fists clench.

Roul hauled the body up and over his shoulder and I was grateful I wouldn't have to carry it. They started walking toward the backyard, but I stopped them.

"I need to pick up her things. Feed her cats. Lock up for her." Care for her in the only way I could.

Kragen nodded. "Make it fast. We'll wait beyond the tree line."

I found an outside faucet and washed my hands. I didn't want to leave blood all over her things. I picked up her bag. Her keys were still in the door. I let myself inside, quickly closing the door behind me so none of the cats would escape.

Her house was small, but comfortable. It felt like home—if home had a dozen cats who stared at you from their various perches. The biggest of the bunch, an orange cat I'd seen in the window earlier, sashayed to me and rubbed itself against my legs.

That seemed to unfreeze the others and they all rushed me, some chirping and others meowing with several running from me to the kitchen and back again.

I chuckled. "Yes, you're hungry. Let me see what I can do."

The first cabinet I opened was full of containers and cans neatly labeled with names like Catticus Finch and Purrito Supreme. I looked at the swirling mass of fur at my feet and sighed. "I hope you know which of you is which."

I picked up a dozen bowls from the floor and set them on the counter. Putting cans of food into them and adding various powders from matching labeled containers was easy. I kept the bowls in the order they were in on the floor and filled them according to the order in the cabinet, before placing them back on the floor.

All the cats lined up at their bowls, some going around others. I hoped that was a sign that they knew who got which bowl. Her disappointment if I made one of them sick would kill me.

I found my brothers in the woods, and we walked to the compound in silence. My house appeared first. I veered to go inside but Drym stopped me.

"What did it feel like when you saw her?"

A low rumble started in my chest. "Like I never wanted to let her go."

He nodded and turned his attention to the backs of the others as they continued to their own houses. Roul splintered from the group, taking the body somewhere no one would find it.

"I think she may be your mate."

My mouth fell open. "My mate?"

"He nodded. If that's the case, you'll need to show yourself. And if she's in danger, you need to do it sooner rather than later."

I shook my head. "She will run and scream. I will terrify her."

He tilted his head. "We didn't terrify Kendal."

My mouth shut with a snap. "Kendal is different."

He shrugged. "You won't know unless you try."

I sighed. "Even if she reacts well, I am broken, Drym."

He shook his head. "You are not. Damaged, yes, but not broken." He walked away, leaving me the one place I didn't want to be. Alone with my thoughts.

SEVEN

I INSTANTLY REGRETTED the decision to open my eyes. The sun had moved into my house and hung out on my ceiling. I didn't think the sun was bright white, but I had to have been wrong. Light filtered red through my eyelids in testament to how bright it was.

I opened my mouth and it felt like I'd tried to eat an entire bag of cotton balls. Or an entire sleeve of Saltines like that internet challenge.

Someone grabbed my hand. Who was in my house? Had to be Emma. She was the only other person who had a key.

"You're okay. You're in the hospital."

"Hospital?" I croaked.

"Here's some water."

I cracked an eyelid a sliver and managed to get the bendy straw into my mouth. I moaned when ice cold water flowed down my throat. As I drained the industrial sized mug, she explained.

"My name is Kendal. I'm a friend of the wyr… man who rescued you."

"That was a woman?"

She chuckled. "No, sorry. I … got distracted by a nurse outside."

That made sense. I'd mashed up phrases I meant to say before. Like thanks and it was nothing ended up coming out thanks for nothing.

"Anyway, the doctors think you have a mild concussion and say they'll release you soon. Do you have someone who can sit with you for a while?"

That was mild? It didn't feel mild. I sighed. "What time is it?" My stomach plummeted as I remembered Sir Purrs-a-lot in the window. "My cats. I have to feed my cats."

"My friend fed them while we were on our way here. He said everything was labeled, so you made it easy."

My entire body slumped. "Thank you."

"Of course. We wouldn't leave them hungry. And it's three in the morning."

"Then no, I don't." Emma would kill me if I woke her up at three a.m. She was not a morning person.

"I know I'm a stranger, but I could stay, if you want. I promise I'm not a serial killer."

"Isn't that what a serial killer would say?"

She laughed. "Probably." Her voice turned serious. "My friend will guard you with his life. Even from me."

I squinted at her. "That doesn't sound like much of a friend."

She smiled. "He's the best kind of friend, believe me."

"Will I get to meet him?"

"I hope so."

"I know I have a concussion, and my brain might not be working well, but you are confusing the shit out of me right now."

She chuckled. "I'm sorry. It's just…" She looked up at the ceiling for a long moment before her eyes met mine. "He's very scary looking, and the last thing he wants is for you to be afraid of him. He's scared that's going to happen."

"Oh." I wasn't quite sure what to say to that, so I closed my eyes and focused on the low hum of the equipment in the room. "Have the police been here?"

"They're waiting outside to take your statement." I heard her clothes rustle as she shifted in the chair. "This is a lot to ask of you, and you don't know me from Adam, but I would really appreciate you not mentioning my friend. It would be fine if you did, eventually, for us, but…" She sighed. "The world we live in is very different, and mentioning him will draw you into it faster than I think you want."

I popped my eyes open. "What, are you in the mafia or something?"

"No! Nothing like that."

"Super-secret government organization?"

Her face brightened. "Yes! That, pretty much."

I fell back on my impossibly thin pillow and regretted that decision when my head hit the hard hospital mattress. I whimpered as pain exploded behind my eyes. "Fine. I'll keep your scary friend to myself. I've already witnessed a murder this week. The last thing I want to do is get caught up in some secret government bullshit."

I heard the door open as the last word left my mouth. I didn't bother sitting up. It was all I could do right then to keep the meager contents of my stomach where they belonged.

"Colorful language for a kindergarten teacher."

"I'm not at work, am I?"

"You're going to come in hot with judgment when she's the victim?"

I wanted to cheer for Kendal, but it would hurt my head.

The man cleared his throat, and I risked raising one eyelid to get a look at him. He had starched his uniform to within an inch of its life, and his shiny badge made me groan and shut my eye.

"Apologies, Ms. Massey. I'm Officer Phillips of Damruck P.D. I'm here to take your statement, if you're feeling up to it."

I spun a finger in a circle. "Fine."

"Can you walk me through what happened tonight?"

"I was unlocking my front door when I felt something behind me. When I turned around, a man said, "Bitch," and hit me on the side of the head." I took a deep breath. "After that, everything gets hazy."

"What were you doing before unlocking your door?"

"Walking up to the door?"

I heard his eye roll. "Before that?"

"After work, I went to Big Muddy's for a burger and fries."

"The one on Mudflats Boulevard?"

"That's the one."

"And then what?"

"Then I drove home. Gathered my things, got out and walked to the door."

He was quiet, so I peeked at him. He scratched furiously at a tiny notebook. Why did cops use such small notebooks? They weren't stiff enough to provide a suitable writing surface and if anyone needed to write in odd places where a good, stiff-backed notebook would be handy, it was cops. Plus, it was so small you could probably only fit one or two words on a line. Unless your handwriting was very cramped.

"How is your handwriting?"

Both Officer Phillips and Kendal looked at me, then at each other.

"Do you want to grade my penmanship?" Officer Phillips studied the tiny notebook for a minute before turning it around for me to see.

The words swam on the page, but I could see that his handwriting was, indeed, cramped. At least it was neat. "B-plus. But actually, I wondered why you don't carry larger, sturdier notebooks that would let you write more and provide a portable writing surface."

He stared at the small pad of paper. "You have a point." He shrugged. "These fit in our pockets, though." He cleared his throat and hovered his pen over the paper. "Back to last night's events. Did you see anyone following you? Notice anything unusual when you got to your house?"

"No. Everything seemed normal until the man appeared behind me and whacked me in the head."

"Can you describe the man? Height, weight, skin color? What was he wearing?"

The man's face flashed in my mind, and I winced. "Average height. Slender, but strong. Caucasian. Brown eyes. He had on a black sweatshirt and dark jeans." I tapped my finger on the bed. "There was something else…" Images flashed through my mind like slides in a projector. They came to a screeching halt on one where my field of vision was mostly filled with concrete steps, but a swath of bright orange stood out. "Orange shoes. He was wearing bright orange shoes. The canvas ones."

Phillips nodded. "You have an excellent memory. That's very helpful. Can you think of any reason someone would want to hurt you?"

"Well, I did witness a murder two days ago. The detectives said I wasn't in any danger from it, though."

"That's probably true, but it's certainly an angle we'll need to explore."

There was that word again. Probably. It was probably a robbery gone bad. I was probably safe. The attack last night probably wasn't connected. My head throbbed in time with my heartbeat.

"Are we done, Officer Phillips? I'd like to rest now."

"Of course. If you think of anything else…." He slipped his card onto the tray table, nodded to both of us, and left.

Not long after, there was a steady stream of health care professionals in and out of my room, making the rest I craved impossible. Nurses came to check my vitals, a general physician came to check on my condition before a neurologist came and declared me fit for discharge. A different nurse came and went over instructions with Kendal. I'd need to be watched for at least twelve hours, preferably twenty-four.

Before I knew it, we were in a large panel van headed to my house. I felt strung up like a harp when we pulled into the driveway. Kendal glanced over at me and must have noticed the strain on my face.

"You can stay at my house if you don't want to stay here."

I gave a tiny shake of my head. "No. My cats are here. I'll be fine once I get inside." I turned toward her. "You don't have to stay. I can call my friend Emma in an hour or two."

"Nonsense!" She grinned. "I sat at the hospital with you. We're practically sisters."

I smiled. Somewhere in the tapioca that was my brain, I knew I shouldn't trust her so fast. She could rob me blind while

I slept. Finish the job the man came there to do. She could be a horrible person.

But I'd learned to listen to my intuition, and right now it was telling me she was good people.

Another slide clicked forward in my brain projector and a warm feeling of safety washed over me. "Did your friend lie down with me?"

"Yeah, he did. He said you were shivering, and he knew he shouldn't move you, so he snuggled up to your back."

I closed my eyes and took a deep breath. "Do you think," I cleared the sudden frog in my throat, "do you think he would come? Just while I sleep. I don't know why, but I'd feel better with him here. I don't have to see him. I promise to keep my door shut and my couch is pretty comfy. I have great blankets and pillows." My ramble trailed off.

She put her hand on my forearm until I looked at her. "I think he'd love that."

EIGHT

I STARED AT my phone screen as my body flashed hot, then cold, then hot again. Kendal's text was only four words, but it short-circuited my brain.

Jade wants you here.

I wanted to run to her, wrap her in my arms and tell her nothing would ever happen to her again. Knowing she would run screaming from me turned my feet to concrete. An impossible weight my legs could never overcome. I was built for shadows and she was the sun.

Ideas swirled in my mind, rejected as fast as they formed.

Before I knew what I was doing, I was dialing Zeus. The owner and leader of Superhuman Security, Zeus had helped integrate us into Supernatural Society shortly after we escaped the lab that created us. He answered on the second ring.

"Thurl. Is everything okay?"

"Yes. No." I rubbed my palm over my scarred eye. "There's a woman. I helped her. Now she wants me to sit with her only…"

"Only she hasn't seen you."

I nodded, realized he couldn't see me, and made a noise of confirmation.

I heard a chair squeak as he sat and sighed. "How can I help?"

"I'm not sure. I can't think. I don't know what to do. Drym believes she may be my mate."

"That certainly complicates things. If she were just a random woman in trouble, I could send one of my guys to pose as her protector."

I growled and startled at the noise.

Zeus chuckled. "And that's why that won't work." The chair squeaked again. "Thurl, I know this is scary, but you're going to have to show yourself. If the meeting goes sideways, call me and Supe Sec will deal with it. But if she really is your mate, then she'll accept you. The fates wouldn't have it any other way."

I grunted through the fear that closed my throat. Memories of women, naked and huddling in the corner of my cell flooded my senses. I could hear their whimpers, see their fear written in every bone and muscle.

The times the scientists put women in with us to see how we'd react were the worst. Especially for me and Roul—the biggest among us.

I didn't want her to look at me like that. I didn't want to scare her, and I didn't see how it would be possible not to. She was human. She had no idea supernaturals existed—much less ones who look like me. There was no camouflage for us. We couldn't hide under a too-big hoodie or shroud ourselves in capes. The hoodie I wore when I killed her attacker only masked my shape and gave me a pocket for my phone. If I hadn't been moving fast, she would have seen my horns, my fur, my muzzle, my claws.

I shook my head to clear it and opened the group text to my brothers.

Jade is asking for me. Zeus told me to go, but revealing myself concerns you, too.

Drym: She's your mate, Thurl. It had to happen at some point. Better sooner than later.

Quin: Wait, what? Cat lady is your mate? How the fuck did that happen?

Kragen: Not something we need to focus on right now, Quin. What else did Zeus say?

Reinar Hilbertson, or Zeus as everyone called him, was also this region's Society representative. He was responsible for making sure the supernaturals of Damruck and surrounding areas followed the rules—and kept out of human sight.

He said to call him if things go sideways.

Kragen: I say go. Give her a chance. We can trust that Zeus has our back.

I watched as one by one, all five of my brothers told me to go to her. I sent a text to Kendal, letting her know I was on my way.

I walked with my heart full of wasps and my head repeated inane words as I thought through what to say. *Hi, I killed the guy who dared to touch you? No one will ever hurt you again? Oh, and by the way, I'm a Wyrfang. A socially and emotionally stunted lab experiment who is touch-starved and possibly crazy.*

And I'm near blind in one eye.

How in the hell could this ever go right?

Full dark settled over the forest as I stared at the back of her house. The enormous orange cat from before jumped into the window and I swore I could hear it call me a coward. I took a deep breath, shook my entire body, and checked that my new set of claw caps were secure for the fifth time.

I made it all the way to the door before freezing again. I stood there and talked myself into leaving. Before I could turn, the door opened and revealed Kendal's smiling face.

"Thought you might need some help getting through the door."

I tilted my head as I searched the frame for hazards.

She laughed. "It's a figure of speech." She grabbed my hand and pulled me inside the warm kitchen that smelled of sugar and sunshine.

I shook my head and pulled back, surprised she kept her grip. "I don't think this is a good idea."

Kendal's grin was impossibly wide. "It's the best idea."

From deep in the house, I heard her voice.

"Kendal? Is that your friend?"

Before I could slap my palm over her mouth Kendal answered.

"Yes."

"Do I need to stay in my room? I promise I won't peek. I don't want you to be uncomfortable."

I gave Kendal a head tilt.

She answered me in a whisper. "I told her you were scary looking and nervous about how she'd react. She offered to let you stay hidden."

My ears pricked at the idea, but before I could nod Kendal called out, "Nope. You can come out!"

"Oh, good."

Did I hear relief in her voice, or was that wishful thinking? I sank onto my haunches, tucking my arms against my belly and tucking my head to my chest. Even as small as I could be, I would be taller than her.

Kendal gave me a soft smile of encouragement.

Jade came around the corner into the kitchen, her face obscured by a towel as she rubbed it in her hair. "Hi. Sorry, I just got out of the—"

She stumbled to a stop and froze; her face a blank mask, her eyes wide. The towel fell from her fingers and her wet hair dropped into her face. Her mouth was open, and I could hear her breathing, but everything else had gone still. It was as if someone took a picture and now we were eternally trapped in our positions.

I startled, and Jade jumped when Kendal broke the silence.

"Jade, this is my friend, Thurl. Thurl, this is Jade."

NINE

THE DOCTORS TOLD me I had a mild concussion, but this was one hell of a hallucination. The beast in my kitchen couldn't be real.

My fingers tingled and I dropped my arms, pushed my wet hair off my glasses and closed my eyes. I took a deep breath, filling my lungs with the familiar smell of my house. I was home. I was safe. My new friend Kendal was standing by my stove. And there absolutely was *not* a massive creature hunched on my floor.

I opened my eyes, but the scene hadn't changed. Whatever it was still crouched on my floor, clearly apprehensive and ready to bolt.

It was hard to make out details in the dim stove light. The overhead fluorescent tube should have been replaced a long time ago, but I never seemed to get around to it. Dark gray fur covered its body. Its eyes shone red. A white scar ran through its eye, down the side of its face, curving to a stop at the corner of its muzzle.

Its arms were wrapped around its middle, its back hunched forward but I could tell its chest was broad and those arms were powerful from the hard muscle evident just under the skin.

As I stared, it seemed to try to make itself even smaller. My heart kicked in my chest and I swallowed. I glanced at Kendal, who was smiling. My instincts told me this creature was more scared of me than I would ever be of it. There was no danger here.

To us, anyway.

My voice came out in a squeak. "Hello."

Its—no, it was definitely a he—his voice was barely more than a whisper. "Hi."

"You…" I cleared my throat and tried for more confidence. "You saved me."

He nodded and my eyes caught on wicked looking horns rising from his skull. I took a step back and his eyes cut to Kendal.

"This was a bad idea. I should go."

She laid a hand on his arm. "Just wait. You're a lot to take in. Give her a minute."

He resumed his efforts to squeeze himself into a small ball.

"You're very brave."

His head tilted as he studied me, his confusion clear on his features.

I nodded. "I know you're scared, and it took a lot to come here. Out of the shadows."

Whisker McFluff darted into the kitchen and rubbed against his legs, purring louder than I'd ever heard. He unwound one arm and gently stroked the cat with two of his fingers. I snorted a nervous giggle when I realized his claws were covered in larger versions of the silicone caps I used to keep the more vigorous scratchers' damage to a minimum.

His head swiveled to the other side.

"Your claw caps are quite handsome."

He lifted his hand and inspected the glittery purple coverings. "Thank you. Kendal makes them for us."

"There are more of you?" My voice was shaky and I fell against the wall.

He shifted and his hands reached for me but stopped short.

Kendal took charge of us both. "Why don't we go into the living room where Jade can sit down?"

She ushered me to my couch and I watched him shuffle after us, keeping himself small. He reminded me of a domesticated former feral cat—skittish and prone to bolt in any new situation. I tucked my legs under me and relaxed into the back cushions.

"You can stand up, you know. You don't have to crouch."

His eyes swung from me to Kendal and back again. He stood, and I was grateful my house had nine-foot ceilings. He still had to keep his head tucked to his shoulders so he didn't skewer the drywall with his horns. His hands opened and closed, and he shifted his weight from foot to foot.

"What *are* you?" My hand flew to cover my mouth as soon as the words were out. "I'm so sorry. That's terribly rude of me."

"No, it's a reasonable question."

His voice rolled over me like thunder, and goosebumps covered my skin. I watched as he settled himself on the floor. His palms rubbed over his knees and the muscles in his forearms and biceps rippled. Someone call a hearse, because I wanted to pet this clearly dangerous beast.

"I am one of six Wyrfangs. A creature made rather than born from a mix of werewolf, wolf, and dragon DNA."

"Um… werewolf and dragon?" I looked at Kendal, wondering if this was some kind of joke. I mean, obviously he was real, and unlike anything I knew of in existence, but werewolves and dragons? They expected me to believe that?

Kendal bobbed her head with a smile. "I wouldn't have believed it myself if I hadn't seen it with my own eyes. There's a whole other world that's full of supernaturals living right under human's noses. All of Society kept secret."

"Right. I can't imagine having something like him walking around would go over well." I leaned forward and he shrunk back. I let my hand drop into my lap.

My hand flew to my mouth and I gasped. "You're the animal, aren't you? You've been watching me."

His muzzle dipped in response.

My belly erupted in butterflies. I stood and paced the small confines of my living room. His eyes tracked my movement.

"Why were you watching me?"

"I … I don't know."

"I've seen you outside for at least a week. You must have some reason."

His eyes cut to Kendal and back to me. "I couldn't sleep, so I took a walk. I heard you calling for Whiskers and I was drawn to your voice."

I watched his chest rise and fall with a deep inhale.

"You smell so good. You looked sad or scared, and I wondered what was troubling you. I wasn't going to come back, but I couldn't seem to stay away." His head dropped. "I'm sorry."

Something propelled me forward and I laid a hand on his massive shoulder. I felt a shudder before he tilted his head and rubbed his cheek on my hand.

A flood of desire washed over me and I stumbled back. He cringed at my sudden movement.

"I'm sorry, I'll go."

I didn't even let him stand up. "Wait!"

TEN

I STARED AT her, not moving a muscle. She bit her bottom lip between her teeth, the pillowy flesh turning bright red in protest. I wanted to soothe it with my tongue. Another shudder rolled through my body.

When she'd touched me, it felt like heaven. I wanted to cover her body with mine, warm her in my arms and shield her from anything that thought to hurt her again. Then she pulled back and my world crashed at my feet. I wanted to say I'd wait for her forever. I would stay right where I was until I turned to ash, but I was too afraid to speak. I didn't want to spook her.

"Um..." She glanced at the floor, at Kendal, at me, and then at the cats rubbing themselves against me. She giggled and waved her hand. "They seem to like you."

"They're soft." I winced as one of them climbed my back, its tiny claws spearing through my fur. It sat on my shoulder. "I like them."

"Me too."

What was this swirl of heat in my gut? Why did my skin prickle when she spoke to me with her voice low and her eyes kind?

"Can you..." She cleared her throat and looked away. "Would you stay tonight?" Her cheeks turned bright red. "I feel safer with you here."

My body lurched forward before I caught myself. Wrapping her tight in my arms wasn't what she asked for. I looked at Kendal, whose grin split her face as she nodded encouragement.

"Yes, I'll stay."

Jade stared at me and the rest of the world fell away. I dimly heard Kendal saying she was headed home, but my focus never wavered. When the door shut, I looked away. "I'll just... lay down here, if that's okay?"

The red tint crept into her upper chest. "Would you stay with me? In my room, I mean. You can sleep on the couch if you'd be more comfortable. I have great blankets and soft pillows. I don't want to make you uncomfortable." She took off her glasses and rubbed her eyes. "I just… I'd like it if you'd hold me."

I was struck dumb. I couldn't speak, couldn't breathe, couldn't move. She wanted me to hold her?

She snorted. "No, of course you don't want to do that. I'm sorry."

She squeaked as I swept her up in my arms and cradled her. "There is nothing I want more."

Her sugar scent turned spicy, a sweet heat that made my cock press at my seam. My pelvis locked. I refused to let it out. She hadn't run yet, but she would, if she saw how much I wanted her. I was already walking when she pointed down the hall. I knew where her bedroom was from the nights I stood outside her window, listening to her sleep.

Gods, I was such a creep.

I laid her down on the soft comforter and she popped right back up. I fisted my hands in dismay. "I'm sorry."

She looked over her shoulder at me, her brows drawn down. "Why?"

I waved at the bed. "You didn't want to be there."

She laughed, and my heart took flight.

"I just wanted to pull the covers back."

"Oh. Right. I'm not used to this yet."

"What? Being with me?"

I tilted my muzzle to the floor. "Sleeping in a bed."

I heard her sharp intake of breath, and I braced for a slew of questions.

They never came.

I looked up as she slid back under the covers and patted the sheets next to her. I circled around and sat carefully on the edge. Her bed was smaller than mine, and I worried it wouldn't hold me. When nothing creaked or snapped, I lowered myself next to her.

She giggled as the bed sank, sending her rolling into me. I buried my nose in her hair and pulled her tight to my body. She let out a happy sigh and put her hand on my chest.

"You're so warm."

My growl sounded more like a purr.

"Thank you. For staying."

There was nowhere else I'd rather be.

ELEVEN

HE WAS GONE when my alarm went off. I might have convinced myself it was all a dream if the smell of him didn't permeate the room. Earthy and warm. I pulled the sheets to my nose and inhaled.

My clit clenched.

It had been a long time since I'd been with anyone. I told myself it was fine, since I had a battery-operated boyfriend in my nightstand, better than any man I'd known. The way my body responded to Thurl made a liar of me.

I snickered. Although I guess I might not be lying, since Thurl was definitely not a man.

I was so turned on lying in his arms the night before that my underwear was soaked through.

That was weird, wasn't it?

He was huge, and scary, with his wicked looking claws (even if they were covered in sparkly purple silicone) and sharp horns. Rationally, I knew the man who attacked me was no longer alive, and that Thurl had killed him.

But all I felt was safe.

Yep, that was weird.

I should probably check myself in for a mental health evaluation. I felt sane, but I was clearly becoming one of those women who write love letters to serial killers in jail.

How many people had he killed? It looked easy for him, so surely that wasn't his first time.

Did I care?

I examined my emotions and found that no, I did not. And what did that say about me? I shook my head. I wasn't going to get anywhere with my thoughts. Best if I got dressed and went to work like it was any other day and I hadn't just spent the night with a monster.

A warm monster who was gentle with me and made me feel safe. Who worried about how I'd react when I saw him. Who seemed vulnerable despite the wicked weapons he sported.

I sighed and rolled out of bed.

Oscar was in the parking lot when I pulled in thirty minutes late.

"Didn't expect to see you today."

"Why not?"

He snorted. "I still have my police scanner, you know. I heard about the attack."

"Oh, right. Well, the doctors said I have a mild concussion and to take it easy, but they didn't say I had to stay at home. I'd rather be here with my students than moping on the couch watching soap operas."

He glanced at me as we walked inside. "Didn't take you for a soap opera girl."

"I'm not. That's my point. And it's hard to find old episodes of *Perry Mason*."

He grinned. "Well, if you need anything today, holler."

He'd walked me all the way to my classroom. "I will."

His lips turned down. "Anything new with Sophia?"

"No, but she spoke to me last week. That's progress."

I stepped into chaos. The school secretary was waving her hands, trying to get the kids' attention. I'd asked her to cover for me until I could get there, and she was clearly out of her depths. Two of the boys were tearing construction paper into tiny shreds and laughing as they threw them in the air.

Another student had pulled all the books off the shelf and was sitting on top of the pile. One little girl smiled as four of her classmates covered her forearm in colorful artwork. Thank past me for ensuring everything in my classroom was washable.

The relief on the secretary's face when she spotted me was comical.

"Thank you for looking after them for me."

Her hand shook as she pushed a lock of gray hair off her face. "No problem."

Her face and tone made it clear it was an enormous problem. She scurried from the room and I surveyed the damage. Then I clapped twice, and the entire room came to a standstill. The only things that moved were the paper shreds falling slowly onto the floor.

"Take your seats."

The rest of the day was without incident. I still got caught several times with my head in the clouds. Sophia even spoke to ask if I was feeling okay. I felt fine. I just couldn't stop thinking about a seven-foot-tall beast. I wondered if he would come again tonight. The thought made me tingle. Which was absurd.

My brain told me I should be afraid of Thurl, but my body disagreed.

I liked to think I was a rational woman of science. I examined the situation like I would a math problem. Stick to the facts.

Thurl had saved me from an unknown attacker who clearly meant for me not to walk away from our encounter. He was aware his size and appearance were overwhelming and made himself seem as small and as nonthreatening as possible. It was clear he was nervous. He didn't ask for anything from me, and was courteous when I asked things of him.

Ergo, Thurl was one of the good guys.

Or at least, he was, until proven otherwise.

Something clicked in my brain. Like I'd given myself permission to like him, to be attracted to him, no matter his size and appearance. He made me feel safe. It wasn't until he showed up that I realized how unsafe I'd felt, which was ridiculous because of course, I felt vulnerable; I'd witnessed a murder and been attacked at my own front door.

I slid into my car with giddy energy and laughed. I couldn't remember the last crush I had. Probably Dwayne Johnson or Jason Momoa. Apparently, big and buff was my type. It made sense. I wanted someone who could pick me up and do things with my body a smaller man would find impossible. I liked my curves, but readily admitted I was a bigger girl.

I had no sooner pulled into my driveway than an unmarked police cruiser pulled in behind me.

"Ms. Massey?"

Close cropped hair pegged the man as former military, but the slight pooch of his belly told me he'd been a cop longer than he served. His suit was neat but not new. His partner emerged from the passenger side holding one of those useless tiny notebooks.

"Yes."

"I'm Detective Chambers and this is my partner, Detective Drake. We'd like to ask you a few questions about the murder you witnessed. May we come in?"

"Are you allergic to cats?"

Chambers chuckled, but Drake winced.

"No ma'am, we are not."

I nodded. "Come on in." I tried not to let the disappointment show on my face. There's no way Thurl would show with police at my house.

TWELVE

I SMELLED THEM before I heard them and heard them before I saw them. Two men in Jade's living room. My fists clenched and I forced myself to breathe. She wasn't in danger. They sat on the opposite side of the room from her. She spoke with animated hands, the soft drone of her voice through the windows steady.

I could see her clearly through the glass. The back of the men's heads bobbed or shook as they asked her questions.

Sir Purrs-a-Lot sat at her feet, but as she spoke more of her cats gathered around her. They could sense her upset. If the men didn't leave in the next few minutes, I'd have to call my brothers for another cleanup. One they wouldn't be happy about, given these men were human officials.

Didn't matter. They were upsetting Jade, and that was reason enough to split them open. I sat back on my haunches, ready to leap through the door, when they stood up and Jade escorted them to her front door.

"We'll let you know when we're ready for you to come to the station and look at mugshots."

I flew around the house and flattened myself to look around the corner at the front door.

"Okay."

The two men shook her hand and then walked to their car. She didn't wait for them to get in before closing her door.

I stared at the men, committing their faces to memory.

"Have you ever seen anyone with so many cats?"

I growled but cut it off when the older man looked in my direction.

He shook his head. "Thought I heard something." He opened the door and slid into the car. "And yes. I have. My aunt ran a shelter. What, you don't like cats?"

The conversation drowned out by the sound of the engine, and I returned to the backyard. Indecision shuffled me from foot to foot. Did I knock? Wait in the trees like I had before? I shouldn't presume she'd want to see me. I was halfway to the tree line when the back door opened.

"Thurl?"

I whirled around and dug my claws into the dirt to keep from running to her.

"Um… would you like to come in?"

I nodded so fast I almost lost my balance. She smiled, and the knot in my chest eased. I was careful as I made my way inside. I didn't want to nick her door with my horns or scratch her floor with my claws. I should ask Kendal for another set of claw caps for my paws. They hadn't been necessary before, but I'd feel better if all of mine were covered.

"Don't worry, the blinds are closed."

She must have noticed my eyes darting around the space.

"If it will make you feel better, I can turn off the lights."

"Thank you," I croaked, then cleared my throat. "That's not needed, unless you'd like to turn them off."

She shook her head, the small smile and flush to her cheeks warming my skin.

"I'd like to look at you." She looked at the floor. "If you don't mind."

I grinned to let out a fraction of the happiness I felt. "I don't mind." I sat on my haunches. She was such a small thing, no bigger than a whisper.

She stopped a hair's breadth from my chest, her fingers reaching before she pulled them back.

"May I?"

I swallowed hard. "You may do whatever you like to me."

Her eyes went wide, and her chest rose. I closed my eyes and inhaled the heady mix of sweet and spice that clung to her. I wanted to bury my nose in her neck, but I forced myself to stay still.

The barest touch of her fingertips against my chest made me groan. She gasped so I grunted, "Don't stop."

Her hand flattened against me and it was beyond anything I could imagine. Her palm made its way down over my abs and to my side before coasting up, around my bicep and down my arm. My cock strained and I shoved my hand against my seam in a last-ditch attempt to keep it hidden.

My eyes flew open as her hand landed on my forearm, traveled to my wrist, and gently tugged. I groaned and resisted the pull.

"What are you hiding from me?"

Her voice was husky and I swelled to the point of pain. I couldn't hold it any longer, so allowed myself to spring from my seam. My chin hit my chest, and I waited for the scream, the sound of running feet, the sound of her leaving me forever.

They never came. Instead, I heard a gasp that verged on a moan and a whispered, "Holy wow."

My eyes popped open and studied her face. Her tongue darted out to lick at her pink lips. She stared at my cock and it preened for her, twitching its pride at her reaction.

I watched as she drew one fingertip down my length, the spikes on my shaft bowing as she passed.

"How…" She swallowed. "What…?"

I managed to rasp, "Werewolf and dragon DNA."

"Which one gave you these?"

Her fingertip glided over my spikes and my head fell back. "Dragon."

Her hand curled around my cock, her fingers in between the spiral of spikes and she squeezed. I whimpered.

She jumped back like she'd been burned. "Oh my god." She spun around and scooted across the room, staring at the wall in front of her. "Oh my god. Oh my god. I can't believe I just did that. I'm so sorry. I'm not usually like this, I'm just curious and you know how they say curiosity killed the cat. I should be dead a hundred times over." She waved a hand behind her in my general direction. "My only excuse is that I've never seen anything like you." Her voice pitched higher into a squeak. "Anything like *that,* and I just couldn't help myself. I'm actually a pretty tactile person, so I touch a lot of things inappropriately, but that's gotta be the most inappropriate thing I've ever done."

It didn't seem like she was going to lose steam anytime soon, so I broke in with, "Satisfaction brought him back."

She whirled back around, her eyes dipping to my crotch for a millisecond. Thank gods I'd managed to get myself under control and my cock tucked securely behind my seam.

"What?"

Her cheeks were bright red and I ached to touch them and see if they were as warm as they looked.

"That's the rest of the saying. Curiosity killed the cat, but satisfaction brought him back."

"I never knew that."

I grinned at her.

She tilted her head, her brows slashing down. "Are you… are you smiling?"

My hands came up to cover my muzzle. "Yes."

She smiled. "It's cute." She dropped her head. "Fuck. No adult likes to be called cute." She looked back up. "Can we maybe start over? Without all of my embarrassing mishaps?"

"I enjoyed your embarrassing mishaps. Too much, maybe. I almost had an even more embarrassing mishap." I smiled as she laughed.

"Right. Okay, well, I wouldn't blame you if you want to leave and never come back."

My entire body lurched toward her. My growl filled the room as I shook my head. "No. I will stay as long as you allow me. Please. Allow me to stay."

She grinned, her chest rising in a deep inhale. "Yes. I'd like that."

THIRTEEN

I WANTED TO melt into the floor. I was mortified. I had touched his penis! Without permission! I don't know what came over me.

That's a lie.

Desire. Desire came over me. His skin was warm beneath my hand, the fur on his chest short and silky, the fur on his sides, upper arms and forearms long enough for me to spear with my fingers. I was so wet by the time I realized he was hiding something with his hand, my brain never registered where his hand was. I'm not sure even if I had clocked that it was covering his crotch I would have stopped.

I wanted to see what he was packing. And whoo boy.

He was packing a huge dick with semi-rigid spikes spiraling down the length. His entire dick was a cock ring. Not one of those you get from a twenty-five-cent vending machine in a truck stop bathroom, but a fancy one you have to order online or get in a store if you're brave enough.

For the record, I've never been brave enough. My vibrator is the plain kind. No bells and whistles because I was too embarrassed to order anything more exciting.

And now all the excitement I could ever want was sitting in front of me, looking for all the world like he'd offer himself up as a sacrifice if I said the word. Why was it so tempting to tell him to ravish me? Why was I feeling this way?

I must have said the second part out loud. Either that or he could read my mind.

"I think it has to do with you being my mate."

"Your what now?" My entire body swayed toward him and I pressed my back against the wall.

He was trying to make himself small again. I didn't want him to.

"Don't hide from me. When you shrink away like that it makes me think you're scared of me." He opened his mouth but I stopped him with a palm. "I know it's because you don't want me to be afraid of you, but I'm not. So stop trying to make yourself small."

It took him a minute to close his mouth. I tended to have that effect on people. His ears flapped back and forth when he shook his head like he was throwing off water.

"My mate. Both dragons and werewolves have fated mates. The one person they're meant to be with. My brother thinks you might be mine."

"Why does he think that?"

"Because of the way I describe how I feel about you."

"How would he know what it feels like?"

"Kendal is his mate."

"So you're what, stuck with me forever?"

He chuckled, but I wasn't seeing anything funny. He probably didn't want to be tied down to one person. Certainly not a chubby kindergarten teacher who had too many cats.

"*If* you accept me and we complete the bond, then I will be the luckiest creature on the planet. But neither of those is an absolute certainty."

I nodded like I understood. I got the basics. It was the details I lacked. Details I wasn't sure I wanted at that moment. I rubbed between my eyebrows as exhaustion crept in.

He stood and scooped me into his arms like I was a penny.

"You are tired. I will put you in bed and leave you alone. We can talk more tomorrow."

He tucked me under the covers but when he went to pull away I stopped him. "Will you stay again? I promise not to assault you in your sleep."

He gave me a grin full of sharp teeth and nodded before settling behind me. A heavy arm draped over my side, his forearm snuggled between my boobs, and his giant hand resting under my cheek.

Thurl could have been a eunuch and I'd still have fallen a bit in love with him that night.

FOURTEEN

I CREPT OUT of Jade's bed while it was still dark outside. I wished she were in my bed, where we could stay all day without worry of her neighbors seeing me. That was a complication my brothers and I didn't need. Especially given BioSynth was still operational.

The lab that created us—the one we'd destroyed when we escaped—may no longer be standing, but the company was still working. Bull, the tech genius for Superhuman Security, felt sure he was getting close to locating them, but the length of time they'd eluded us was frustrating.

Even if BioSynth was permanently shut down, we couldn't walk the streets in broad daylight. Humans were unaware Society existed, and supernaturals liked it that way. There were too many of us with fearsome appearances or odd dietary needs to coexist nicely with people.

I had experienced firsthand what humans could do when they thought another species was less than or a commodity. Bacon, a Society historian of sorts who worked with Jackal Division, gave us binders as a crash course on Society that detailed more examples. None of which ended well.

With Kendal's help, we hadn't needed to exist in the wider world. She acted as a go-between for all the mundane needs we had. Security systems, fences, and gates secured our compound, a large tract of land with each of our six houses, from the outside world.

Our need to stick to the shadows had never bothered me before. When we ran missions, we borrowed Zeus' private plane and flew at night. The all-supernatural crew didn't bat an eyelash.

Now I wondered if Jade would chafe at the restrictions. She couldn't talk to her coworkers about me. I could only see her at night unless she moved in with me, which presented its own set of problems.

Kendal rarely left the compound. She acted as our property manager. If we added a resident that wished to work outside every day, our security would need to adapt.

I was getting ahead of myself. Jade made me jealous, in more ways than one. I didn't want anyone else to touch her, but I also wanted what Drym had. He was happy with Kendal, but more than that, he was at peace.

His nightmares were gone. He slept through the night, his mind quiet.

Quin's foot tapped the boards of my back porch as I approached, the rhythmic sound keeping time with the swing's back and forth sway. I was halfway across the porch when he spoke.

"Is it true?" Uncharacteristically sad eyes met mine. "Is she your mate?"

"I think so."

He sighed. "I want to be happy for you, but I'm sad I'm losing my brothers."

I joined him on the swing. The wood released an ominous creak, but it held. "You aren't losing us."

"Logically, I know that. You'll still be here. But Drym's changed. He has Kendal. He doesn't need us anymore."

I leaned my head back and thought. Quin was the most emotional of us. He masked his deeper emotions with humor, but I could see he was haunted. He felt responsible for us. Not like Kragen's big brother energy and its need to protect and guide us, but as someone who would save us from despair. He tried hard to keep us smiling, even in the darkest of days.

I always thought it was part of being a healer. I envied his ability to be lighthearted. Now I wonder if it was a burden, the weight of which none of us knew.

"We will always need each other, Quin. We are brothers. We are the only wyrfangs in existence. Our mates don't change that. They are a different need. Our hearts swell large enough to hold them, along with all of you. I don't love you less now that I've found Jade." I snorted. "Besides, I have no idea if she'll accept me."

He put his hand on my knee. "She will."

"Thank you, but I'm not entirely confident."

We sat in silence and listened to the sound of the chain and the birds. He shot to his feet and off the porch, turning when he reached the lawn.

"She will." His tongue swiped at his muzzle. "You're a protector, Thurl. She would be a fool to turn away from you."

My heart clenched in my chest as I watched him walk away.

I knew Quin wouldn't come to me to chase his demons at night anymore. I made a mental note to ask Roul to look in on him.

Roul was difficult and became more so with each day that passed without Victoria. The witch who helped us escape had followed BioSynth after our last encounter with them and took another piece of his soul with her. I didn't think she knew the anguish he felt, not knowing where she was or how she fared.

I couldn't imagine being separated from Jade. I had a greater appreciation for his pain, and my heart broke for him. We would find them. We would get her back. It needed to be soon, before we lost him to madness forever.

I went inside and checked my phone before heading to bed. Kragen had sent me a text.

Bull found out who Jade's attacker was and who he worked for. He'll come to the commons at noon.

It was barely eight in the morning, but I couldn't risk falling asleep and not waking to an alarm. I bypassed my stairs and went out the front, following the path to the structure we used as a gathering place. I settled on the floor, just beyond the door.

There was little chance I'd sleep through my brothers tripping over me when they arrived.

FIFTEEN

SOPHIA HAD RETURNED to being a lump in the corner. It hurt my heart. Something was clearly going on with her, but she didn't trust me enough to talk to me about it. She even went to the cafeteria for lunch with the rest of the kids rather than stay with me.

I sighed as I stared at the lunch I'd packed for a hurting kid. If I ate it by myself, I'd be a raging, sugar fueled pterodactyl by the last bell. I needed protein, but the idea of trudging to the cafeteria and screaming my choices to the lunch ladies over the cacophony of more than one hundred elementary school children was unappealing.

I rummaged through my desk drawers, hoping for something halfway decent, but all I found was Halloween candy I'd confiscated the year before and a granola bar that rattled in its package like it had end-stage emphysema.

I eyed my options and tried to decide what was the least of the evils spread in a sad banquet before me. My phone buzzed and I dove for it. It probably wasn't a notification that I'd won a surprise lunch from my favorite deli, delivered to the office, but a girl could hope.

It wasn't, but it was something almost as good. Detective Chambers requested I visit the station to look through mugshots. He said I could come in anytime, but for the first time in forever, the thought of teaching the second half of the day dragged me down like a kraken.

I idly wondered if kraken were real. Maybe I'd ask Thurl later.

I gathered my things and booked it to the front office, where the secretary didn't bother to hide her wince when I told her I needed to leave for the day. She brightened when I said that I'd arranged a last-minute substitute to take my kids for the afternoon.

The latest Heaving Bosoms podcast blasted through the speakers when I cranked my car. I leaned my head against the headrest and inhaled until my lungs hurt before I steeled my spine and hit the gas. I smiled along as Melody and Sabrina cackled their way through recapping their latest read.

I must not have paused it fast enough when I pulled through Big Muddy's for a burger, since the checkout girl smirked at me. It wasn't the first time the Heaving Bosom's ladies had educated a random stranger about some aspect of smut courtesy of my car audio.

They were sharing their lady loves when I pulled into the police station parking lot. I grabbed my bag and made my way inside. I would have felt better with Thurl holding my hand. I smiled, thinking about the different reactions I would get walking into the police station with a seven foot, heavily muscled monster that looked straight out of an original Grimm fairy tale.

I bet that tough-looking policeman behind the reception desk would pee himself.

I found detective Chambers after being directed to the third floor. He smiled and shook my hand.

"Thank you for coming in, Ms. Massey. This shouldn't take long."

He waved me into a conference room chair and handed me a tablet with six criminals' worst portraits ever displayed on the screen.

"If you tap the pictures, they'll enlarge. Just tap again to go back to the grid. You can swipe left and right to go through more. I've narrowed the field a bit, so if you reach the end and don't recognize anyone, let me know."

"Okay."

"There's coffee that I can't recommend unless you need to remove paint from something, and a vending machine down the hall. I'll be right outside if you need anything."

I chuckled good-naturedly at his joke as he left me alone in the room. I scrolled through photos for fifteen minutes before they ran together. I stood up and stretched. Detective Drake poked his head in the door.

"Are you okay?"

I nodded. "Just needed to give my eyes a break."

His pinched smile made it seem like he needed some Pepto Bismol. I glanced back at the tablet and yelled, "Wait!" before the door even latched.

I felt him behind me as I pointed to one photograph. "That's him!"

Detective Chambers joined us. "Are you sure?"

"I'm sure that is either the man I saw or his doppelgänger."

The two detectives exchanged a cryptic look. Chambers rubbed his eyes.

"What? What are you not saying?"

"That is the head of Silver Fang—an upstart smuggling organization trying to chew trade routes away from The Level, which was the largest criminal syndicate in the area."

"There is organized crime in Damruck?" Although not small enough to be considered a true small town, the city was still not big enough to be considered any kind of metropolitan area. The idea of crime families being in Damruck was kind of like a scuba diver packing crackers for a mid-dive snack.

Drake nodded. "There are currently six crime orgs in the city."

Detective Chambers gave his partner a harsh glare before turning to me with a soft smile. I looked as shell-shocked as I felt. He placed a clammy hand over mine on the table.

"You think my attack from the other night is related? Now that you know who I witnessed killing someone, you think this crime boss has figured out who I am and has already sent someone after me?"

"You're going to be okay. We'll put you under police protection."

Thurl. I didn't need police protection. I just needed to get to the monster who'd been sleeping in my bed.

I cleared my throat. "I don't think that'll be necessary. I have somewhere I can go. It's not connected to me, so there's no way he can find me."

Chambers' brows drew down. "I'd feel better if you stayed under police protection."

My spine stiffened. "Trust me when I tell you I will be far safer than with any protection detail you could provide."

His skeptical frown lasted long enough to make my skin itch. I broke through his thick fog of disapproval with a question. "What happens if I refuse to testify?"

I wouldn't. My sense of justice was too strong to let the weasel get away with killing what amounted to a kid. But I needed to know the possibilities.

Chambers sighed and leaned back in his chair. "Then he'll most likely walk. Adrian Vale is charming and cunning in equal measure. He also has enough wealth to hire the best attorneys. We've been trying to get him on something for years, but he wiggles free each time." He sat forward and stared into my eyes. "That won't keep you safe, Ms. Massey. He will come after you, whether or not you testify. He won't take the risk of leaving you alive."

I blew out a breath. "I understand. I plan to testify. What are the next steps?"

Detective Drake stepped forward. "We'll take your statement and document your identification. Then we turn everything we have over to the District Attorney, who will move forward with prosecution."

Chambers leaned back again. "The process can be lengthy."

"I'll talk to my principal. I'm sure we can work something out." I wasn't sure, and the idea that my career was going to be cut short gutted me. But like I told my kids: you eat the elephant one bite at a time. My next step was getting to Thurl.

In no time at all, I had signed a printed photo of the man I identified as the killer, along with a statement I'd written attesting to that fact. Completely upending my life seemed like it should be more momentous than a couple of scribbles of my name on paper. Where was the ominous thunderclap soundtrack? The floor falling from beneath my feet to mark the occasion?

I glanced out the window on the other side of the space. The sun was setting. I needed to get home. I stood and gathered my things. "You have my cell number if you need to reach me."

Detective Drake opened the door to the conference room and waved me through. "Will you let us escort you home?"

"I'd rather not attract more attention to myself than I already have, but thank you."

I felt Chambers' frown at my back. "If you change your mind about police protection…"

I turned and gave him a smile faker than the Gucci bags being sold on the corner. "You'll be the first to know."

SIXTEEN

"YOUR MATES NEVER do anything in half measure, do they?"

Bull, Superhuman Security's resident tech expert, never looked up from his laptop screen as his fingers flew over the keys.

"What do you mean?" My fists clenched at my sides. I needed to get to her house. To make sure she was safe.

"The dude you sliced and diced works for Silver Fang, one of the crime organizations in the city."

"There is more than one?" Kragen sat forward and I could see his claws marking the table. I winced. Kendal didn't like us marking up the furniture.

Bull made a face. "Unfortunately. There are six known groups working in the area. Silver Fang is bad, but it could have been worse. She could've stumbled into the Red Syndicate's viper nest."

"Why so many? Damruck doesn't seem large enough to support one crime organization, much less six."

I dimly registered Kragen's voice and Bull's response as I seethed with barely constrained rage.

"It's the ley lines. Damruck sits on top of the intersection of two ley lines, which gives it more power than its size warrants. It attracts all sorts of rotten apples. Mostly human, but Society too."

I growled. The idea that Jade was in danger from a papercut made my blood boil. To hear that she might be the target of an entire criminal enterprise made me want to submit to the fog and kill everyone in sight.

Drym punched my bicep. "Look at him. She's definitely his mate."

I snapped my teeth and ripped hair from his forearm.

"No need to get violent." He rubbed his arm and backed away.

Kragen shook his head. “Thurl, go get her. She’ll stay with you until we can ensure her safety.”

Bull whistled, and everyone’s head swung to him. “The police just logged her witness statement. She’s identified the leader himself as the man she saw committing murder.” He glanced up from his screen to pin me with a stare. “Kragen’s right. She’ll be safest with you.”

I wanted to run, but stayed mindful of the floor. I could dig my claws into the dirt outside without upsetting Kendal.

SEVENTEEN

THE PHONE RANG while I struggled with my front door key. I sighed and rolled my eyes as Gwen Stefani spelled bananas and swiped the screen.

"Hi Nanna."

"What's this I hear about you being caught up in police business? Did you ask for a lawyer? Don't ever talk to the police without a lawyer." I heard general noises of agreement from the other ladies in her poker club, along with one shouted "ACAB!" from someone I couldn't identify.

"I don't need a lawyer. I witnessed a murder. How do you know about it?"

"Heard it on the police scanner."

"Of course you did."

"Don't sass me! I shouldn't have had to hear about it on the police scanner. You should have called me."

Tears welled in my eyes. Hearing her voice triggered the meltdown I'd put off for too long. "I haven't had time. It's been kind of crazy."

She made a sound like air leaking from a balloon. "Crazy is my specialty."

It actually was. Nanna came of age in the sixties and embraced the free love, commune lifestyle before making a hard left in the eighties and becoming a corporate power broker. In the nineties, she made another U-turn and went new age, talking me into going with her to Rainbow Family gatherings and Spiral ceremonies. She was a five-foot nothing bulldozer and it didn't matter if she was running you over with love or kicking your ass; you were guaranteed to feel it.

I loved her, but she could be a lot.

I took a deep breath and blinked back the tears. Now was not the time. I needed to pack and wander in the woods until Thurl found me. I would have to call Emma and beg her to take care of the cats for a while. I'd have to take my two extra special needs kitties with me. Sir Purrs-a-lot needed daily medication and refused to let Emma near him, and Catzilla was just mean to everyone but me.

"I know, and ordinarily you would have been my first call, but there are extenuating circumstances this time." Like a seven-foot tall, horned, tailed beast.

"Extenuating circumstances?"

"Yes."

"I'm coming over."

The line went dead before I could make another sound. Nanna's active senior neighborhood was on the other side of the city, but it wouldn't take her long to get here. Mom had tried to take her keys once, saying she was no longer fit to drive. Nanna didn't speak to her for half a decade. Since I lived with Nanna until I went to college, I spent those years acting as go-between. *Tell your grandmother this* and *tell your mother that* got old after the first month, but Nanna wouldn't budge so I got used to it.

I rushed around, hoping to at least be packed before she showed up. I had no idea what I threw into my suitcase, but I carefully packed Sir Purrs-a-lot's meds and enough food for him and Catzilla before corralling them into carriers. I was on the phone with Emma when Nanna's tires squealed as she came around the corner.

The two right wheels barely touched the ground as she whipped into my driveway.

All I wanted was to find Thurl and curl up with him, and I almost lost it when she slid from her land yacht and shuffled at what she called lightning speed (which was slightly faster than a normal walking pace) to where I stood in the living room. She didn't slow down until I was sinking against her impossibly soft bosom and belly while her arms cut off my circulation.

"Thanks so much, Emma. I owe you one."

As soon as I hung up Nanna pushed me back and gave me a once over. "You look okay. Are you okay? Of course you're not okay, that's a stupid question."

I'd learned it was best to wait until she ran out of steam before trying to get a word in. She turned toward my kitchen.

"I'll make cookies. Snickerdoodles. Those are still your favorite, right?"

"Yes, but Nanna—"

"Good. You'll have the ingredients because you're a good girl who learned that keeping emergency cookie ingredients on hand is imperative."

No one would ever go hungry if Nanna could help it. Her door was always open, and more days than not, she had something yummy baking when school let out. I was only popular because nobody wanted to be banned from Nanna's house.

"Nanna, please. You can't stay."

Something in my voice must have registered because she stopped pulling out cookie sheets and turned around. "Why not?"

"The police don't think it's safe for me to stay here, so I'm going to stay with a friend."

She nodded several times before she shoved the cookie sheet back into the cabinet. "I'll go with you. Will they have emergency cookie ingredients, or do we need to stop on the way?"

I winced. This would not go over well. "You can't."

"The hell you say. I can and will. No granddaughter of mine is going into hiding without me."

"I'm your only granddaughter."

She waved her arm. "Beside the point. You've never been in hiding before, and I have. It only makes sense I go with you."

"The friend I'm going to stay with is very private. I haven't even asked if I can stay with him yet, and I doubt he'll want extra guests."

Her eyes narrowed. "Very private?"

I nodded.

"Is that code for supernatural?"

My face gave away my shock.

"Oh, don't look so surprised. I'm eighty-one years old and have depths and multitudes of layers you've only scratched the surface of."

"But how do you know supernaturals exist?"

"I spent an amazing month with a vampire named Killian." She fanned herself. "The things that bloodsucker could do would curl your toes."

"I get the picture!" I needed to cut off that line of conversation before she went into far more detail than anyone wanted to hear. "It still has to be up to him. You can't invite yourself."

"Fine, fine." She plopped onto my couch and patted her lap. Three cats came running to vie for her attention. "Be a dear and grab my go bag from the trunk while we wait."

EIGHTEEN

I WALKED THROUGH the back door into Jade's house and said, "You're staying with me."

Her voice wove over mine. "Can I stay with you?"

We both smiled, and I relaxed a bit. Then a strange woman stepped beside her. Her eyes went round and her jaw slack, but then she grinned and elbowed Jade.

"Please tell me you're hitting that."

"Nanna!" Jade's blush spread to her chest.

"What? If you aren't, I might throw my hat in the ring. You never know, he might have a granny kink."

Jade's head fell back and she stared at the ceiling. "Please stop talking."

The older woman winked at me before she shuffled over and wrapped my waist in a hug. I patted her back. Even with Kendal's daily hugs, I felt awkward.

She backed until she held me at arm's length. "Sit down, boy, and let me get a good look at you."

I fell to my haunches. Despite Jade's reactions to the woman's words, this was clearly someone she cared for. I grunted when she grabbed my horns and yanked my face close to hers. "If you hurt her, I will string your balls from the fence post at the Sunset Springs community center—with you still attached to them."

I swallowed and nodded as much as I could. Her grip was strong and the promise shining in her eyes left little doubt she'd do it.

My eyes flicked to Jade, who was pinching the bridge of her nose, her glasses perched on her forehead.

"Nanna, we need to go."

"Nonsense! You haven't even properly introduced me."

Jade flicked a hand from me to the woman and back. "Thurl, meet Nanna, my grandmother. Nanna, meet Thurl."

I dipped my head. "A pleasure?" I didn't mean to make it sound like a question. Instead of being offended, Nanna laughed.

"Nanna wants to come with me, but you don't have to say yes."

Jade was clearly trying to convey something with the look she gave me, but I couldn't decipher whether it was to allow her grandmother to come or not.

"If you wish it." I would risk my delicate bits being crucified while still attached if it meant Jade was happy.

"Of course she wishes it." Nanna patted my arm. "Be a dear and get my bag."

Somehow, I ended up with two small suitcases and a cat carrier. Jade insisted on carrying the bag of supplies she was bringing for the cats and the other cat, saying he would need time to warm up to me. I didn't know what that meant, but the enormous orange cat seemed happy with me, judging by the loud purring that came from his carrier.

We were a strange, slow parade through the woods. Nanna had kept a steady stream of questions flowing in Jade's direction, but as we stepped onto my porch, she went quiet.

I rubbed at my suddenly itchy arms and tried to see my house through fresh eyes. By the time she spoke, I was ready to tear it down and build whatever Jade wanted.

"What a lovely home."

I went to rub the back of my neck but realized my hands were full of luggage and a cat. "Thank you."

"Where is the kitchen?"

"Umm..." I looked at Jade, who seemed resigned to whatever was coming next. "It's just through that door." I twitched my muzzle to indicate the correct one. Nanna shuffled in that direction while I made my way to the bedrooms.

Jade stepped into the guest room behind me.

"Thank you for letting us stay. Especially Nanna. She can be overwhelming, but she means well."

"She wants to protect you. I respect that." I set her suitcase on the dresser. "Will this be okay?"

Jade nodded. "All I really need is a bed and a bathroom. I can be fancy, but it doesn't happen often, if that makes sense."

It didn't, but I nodded anyway. "The bathroom is here." I opened the door to show her. "There are towels and things in the cabinet. Kendal helped me furnish and stock my house, but if anything is missing let me know."

She turned and looked up at me. "Does she do all the shopping for you?"

There was a note in her voice. Something I couldn't pinpoint. I shook my head. "No, only the items that need to be purchased in person. Most of the time, I order what I need online and they deliver it to the common hall."

"Common hall?"

"It is a shared structure where my brothers and I gather."

"You have more than one?"

I nodded. "There are six of us." I turned and made my way to the next bedroom down the hall. She hadn't pushed me that first night we met, but I knew the questions were coming. Who was I? How was I made? What happened to my eye? All of which would lead to our escape from the laboratory that created us. It was not a tale I relished telling.

I didn't want her curiosity to turn to horror.

"Is this room acceptable for you? It also has its own bathroom, just there."

"Oh."

My ears flattened against my head. I had disappointed her somehow. "I can rearrange the furniture. Change the wall color?"

"It's not that. I'd just…" She sucked in a huge breath. "I'd hoped to stay with you. In your room."

I wasn't normally a chatty creature, but I rarely lacked for words. Until Jade. Every other minute, she rendered me speechless.

I picked up her suitcase and the large orange cat up and strode to my room. It was the largest of the four to accommodate my size, with a custom-built bed. I'd opted for soft sheets and colors, not wanting anything to remind me of the lab. Nothing was stark white. No sharp corners or harsh lights.

Jade gasped beside me. Before I could ask her what was wrong, she'd set down both the bags she carried and taken a flying leap onto the bed. She squealed with delight as she sank into the softness and my heart lit up like a bolt of lightning against a dark sky.

That joy was chased by a wonderful scent hitting my nose. "What is that?" I lifted my muzzle and tried to decipher what I smelled.

Jade sighed happily. "Snickerdoodles."

NINETEEN

THURL'S KITCHEN WAS a chef's dream. Not that I was a great cook, but Nanna was clearly in her element.

It was hard to pry myself from Thurl's bed. It was as comfortable as the sweatshirt I'd stolen from an ex-boyfriend in college. I wouldn't even need covers with Thurl to keep me warm.

Sir Purrs-a-lot's irritated *meow* broke the bed's trance. I set up water and a litterbox before releasing him and Catzilla. They both took up their mission of thoroughly inspecting Thurl's bedroom while we made our way to the kitchen.

Nanna stood in front of the open pantry door, a dreamy look on her face. From what I could tell, both ovens were stuffed full of cookie trays. Apparently, she decided Thurl's size meant he needed three dozen cookies alone.

"How many cookies are you making?" Visions of going door-to-door with buckets of cookies gave me goosebumps.

She turned around and took in Thurl's form with a wave of her hand. "Enough for him and the rest of his pack. Don't worry, I doubt we'll have leftovers." She tapped a finger against her lips. "We might not have enough. I should have made more." She grabbed Thurl's arm. "How many are in your pack?"

"Pack?" My eyes ping-ponged between them until I got dizzy and had to stop.

"Of course, dear. Thurl is clearly of the canine persuasion, and I've never known a werewolf without a pack."

"He's not a werewolf, Nanna." My hand met air behind me as I searched for someplace to plant my butt. She gave me a look that clearly said, *no shit, Sherlock.*

Thurl scooped me up before my ass hit the tile and deposited me in a cushioned chair.

"Wyrfang, actually."

Nanna exclaimed in glee. "I've never heard of you! Oh, this is wonderful. Tell me all about your breed."

Thurl's tongue appeared and disappeared several times as he licked his lips. It was confusing to watch, then became mesmerizing when I realized what I was looking at.

His tongue was *forked.*

I shook my head to clear the rapid mental slide show that discovery initiated and sent a warning glare to Nanna. "I don't think he wants to talk about it."

I'd noticed whenever anything about his past came up, he became uncomfortable. I'd been trying to avoid asking the million questions I had, wanting to wait until he was ready.

His head drooped between his shoulders and his chest rose and fell. "No, it's all right."

His stare pinned me, spread my imaginary wings, and framed me in a display case.

"I am one of six wyrfangs. We were created to be…"

He swallowed and I wanted to hug him, but I couldn't move.

"An elite fighting force. Scientists used werewolf and dragon DNA to craft the perfect weapon for their military contractors. We spent most of our lives in a laboratory, under the constant watch of cameras, performing in dozens of experiments to prove our capabilities."

Nanna and I both wrapped him in a hug. She let go first.

"You poor thing. Call your brothers." She swiped her eyes with the edge of an apron, because of course she packed an apron in her go bag. She didn't own any appropriate ones. Thankfully, that one was relatively mild, reading "Cheese Slut" in a pretty cursive across her boobs. "What do you like to eat? I'll make something you can have after cookies."

He tilted his head. "Cookies are dessert?"

I nodded. "Yes, but Nanna always has dessert first."

"And after. It would be a shame if you died before dessert, or before you could have a little something sweet after dinner."

"Does that happen often? Humans dying during a meal?"

Nanna waved her hands. "No, but better to be safe than sorry, right?"

I leaned over and whispered in his ear, "Just go with it. You'll learn it's almost impossible to understand her—or win an argument against her, for that matter."

Nanna swirled a spatula in our general direction. "Go on then. Invite your brothers to dinner. I'm guessing meat? Of course it's meat."

She started pulling the entire contents of his refrigerator onto the counters, along with half of the things from his pantry.

"Let's go before she kicks us out."

"But I thought she wanted me to invite my brothers?"

"Oh, she does. She won't want us in the kitchen while she cooks, though."

He tossed a worried look over his shoulder as we stepped outside. I patted his arm.

"It's okay. She is a fantastic cook, and one of her favorite things is feeding people. It's one of her love languages."

"Love language?"

I giggled. "Yeah, it's a saying that started a few years ago when someone wrote a book about five love languages. Now it's used to show any way someone shows their love, or prefers to receive it."

"What are the five love languages?"

He looked ready to pull out a pen and paper to take notes, and my middle went gooey. "I know one is physical touch and another is gifts, but I can't remember the rest. To be honest, I never read the book."

"What is your love language?"

His eyes seemed to bore through me and I would have sworn they flared brighter. A trill ran up my spine and I clamped my thighs together. "Um. Cats, I suppose. Love my cats, love me."

His eyes closed like he committed it to memory. He looked away before opening them. "Will you come with me to the common hall?"

"To invite your brothers to dinner?"

"Yes."

I smiled up at him. "Sure."

He took off down a path and I trotted to catch up to him. I tried to sound casual as I asked, "So, what is your love language?"

He spun around and dropped into a crouch in front of me, his eyes definitely blazing red, the scarred one a touch dimmer than the other.

"You."

His voice was deeper than I'd ever heard, and the growl of it washed over my skin like a rough caress. I swallowed hard. I reached for him without thought and he gently took my hand in his giant one, curling his fingers around mine.

How did such a massive, deadly creature become so gentle?

"We are all gentle."

I startled, not realizing I'd asked out loud.

"Except for maybe Roul." He snickered. "But Jade?"

"Hmm?"

"Make no mistake. The scientists did their jobs well. We are killers. And I *will* kill anyone who threatens you."

I was going to have to carry a spare pair of panties unless I wanted to walk around in wet ones all day.

TWENTY

I TRIED TO ignore the smell of Jade's arousal. We were nearly to the common hall. If we were slightly further away, I'd be tempted to pull her into the woods and see how far she would take her curiosity.

I didn't think it was anything more than that. She looked at me like the scientists did—only with far more heat. She hadn't been able to help but touch me. Even that small contact had me wanting to crawl out of my skin and into hers. My willpower was stretched to its limit, but I would stay in control. For her.

I opened the door to the hall and nearly ran into her as she stopped just inside. She took a step back, putting her back flush to my front and my hand instinctively wrapped around her, shielded her, protected her. I growled at the room and my five brothers stopped talking, their heads swiveled toward us in unison.

Roul stepped back and crouched. He and I were the muscle of our group, and well aware of our size.

Not to say the rest weren't fearsome. All of them, save Drym, made themselves smaller. Drym's head rested on top of Kendal's, arms wrapped around his mate much as mine were wrapped around Jade.

It wasn't unusual for all of them to be here. We gathered around this time every day, and most preferred to spend most of their time here. As Quin said, it was strange still to be alone.

Kendal broke the tension. "Jade! How are you?"

I felt Jade's head move against my chest as she surveyed the room.

"I'm okay. A bit overwhelmed, to be honest. This is…"—her forearm muscles bunched under my arm as she waved her hand—"a lot. I don't know what I was expecting. I knew there were six of you. I just didn't think you'd all be as scary as Thurl, I guess. I'm sorry, that's presumptive of me. You're probably all marshmallows." She sucked in a breath. "Sorry, I talk when I'm nervous. I'll shut up now."

Kragen chuckled and I felt the need to tear him apart until I saw he wasn't laughing at her.

"It's all right. We are a lot to take in. I don't know that I'd call us marshmallows, but I guarantee you have nothing to fear from us."

"Good, yes, that's great." She tilted her head toward my chest and whispered, "Don't let go, okay?"

I felt my voice vibrate through her. "Never."

She relaxed and so did I, finally stepping together through the door.

I waited as my brothers introduced themselves and their roles in our small group. Kragen, our leader, went first, followed by Drym, his second in command. They were the brains of our unit. Roul and I were the brawn. I specialized in weapons and acquiring them. Roul was the best at hand-to-hand combat and infiltration. Cavi was our doctor and Quin served as field medic.

Silence fell once everyone had given Jade their name until she cleared her throat. "Um, I hope you guys are hungry. Nanna insisted on coming with me and she's cooking what I suspect is everything in Thurl's house at the moment. She's invited you all to dinner."

Kragen's head tilted. "Are you okay with us coming to dinner? It will be tighter quarters."

She seemed to think about it for half a second before nodding. I heard the smile in her voice.

"Who else is going to eat all that food?"

I kept a close eye on Jade as we walked back. We stayed at the back of the group. I didn't want her to feel the weight of them behind her. I kept my hand curled around her shoulders, and she gripped my finger tight in her fist.

She shook her head. "How did they keep you for so long?"

I wasn't sure she meant to ask aloud, but I answered her. She deserved to know our story. "They constantly monitored us. If scientists weren't present, there were cameras watching our every move. Any outside missions were done with heavy artillery pointed at us. Trackers were implanted beneath our skin. It was made clear there was no way to escape."

"How did you escape?"

"One scientist saw what they were doing and knew it was wrong. She's a witch, and helped us escape."

"I hope you burned the lab when you got out. Are the scientists in jail?"

It was probably an unconscious move, but her fist left my finger and dug into the fur of my forearm. I moved my arm lower so she wouldn't have to reach behind her so far. I encouraged any touch she'd give me. I might lose it completely with my next answer.

"They are dead."

TWENTY-ONE

I SHOULD HAVE known. These beasts who had such horrible things done to them their whole life wouldn't leave their torturers alive.

What shocked me was how good I felt knowing they were dead. How relieved that they were gone and wouldn't trouble them anymore.

I could feel Thurl tense behind me.

"Good. I'm glad they're dead and can't hurt you anymore."

He melted into me, and I sank into his side.

"The organization still exists. They continued without us, and I'm sure they still look for a way to retrieve us."

"You can't track them?"

His muzzle dipped and his eyes closed. His chest rose and fell twice before he answered. "We are looking. There are others who are helping us, but so far, they remain elusive."

I chewed on my lower lip. In such a short time, I'd come to care about Thurl. Maybe it was the mate thing causing me to fall a bit in love with him every minute. Could I ask if it affected me in this way? *Hey, Thurl, does me being your mate make me want to mash our parts together? Does it make me love you?* Was there a way to ask without sounding like a total ninny?

I still hadn't worked it out when we arrived back at his house. The rich smell of meat wafted from the open door. A few of the other wyrfangs raised their noses to the air, some licked their lips, and others made noises of obvious approval.

Nanna appeared on the porch. "Oh my, look at y'all."

Little cartoon birds and hearts floated around her face. I thought about warning them, then decided they could take care of themselves.

"Well, don't just stand there, come inside and set the table."

She disappeared, and her troops followed the general obediently. By the time Thurl and I squeezed into the dining room, she had given each of the others a task, and they moved with precision to lay out plates, cups, and silverware.

I spotted Kendal as she held up the wall and tried to stay out of the way. I pressed through the wall of muscle to her side.

"Thank you."

She looked over without her bemused smile faltering. "What for?"

"For making sure this house was stocked with everything to make this possible." I waved at the controlled chaos that had moved from dinnerware to a well coordinated wait staff ferrying platters and serving bowls overflowing with food to the table.

She sighed. "I had hoped to see this one day. Aside from the first few weeks, they've tried to eat separately. Some are more successful than others. I think they believe they need to be independent, but they need each other. It hasn't been a simple transition to freedom. So I should actually thank you."

"Not me. This is all Nanna's doing." My grandmother's bright grin must be visible from the moon. She was in her element and loving every second.

"Your Nanna is the best. I think she'll be good for the 'fangs." Kendal looked over the wyrfangs as they did an old lady's bidding. "Everyone needs a kind grandmother figure, don't you think?"

I laughed. "Probably, but I'm not sure she fits the stereotype. She's more of a tiny terror, but she's the best. And she's already adopted them." I pointed into the kitchen where Nanna was standing in the center of a ring of wyrfangs, swatting some on the arm and hugging others as she handed out snickerdoodles.

It didn't take long for me to feel comfortable around them. When we sat down and started to eat I watched them interact and their personalities shone through. Kragen was a calming presence. Quin was the complete opposite—a total goofball who delighted in making everyone laugh. Cavi was quiet, but observant. Drym was focused on Kendal and seemed happy. Roul sat sullen, hardly speaking.

Nanna took a special interest in Roul. I wasn't sure if that was good or bad for him, but having her focused elsewhere lifted a bit of pressure from me. I watched carefully for most of dinner to make sure he wouldn't tire of her, but his patience seemed endless.

She continually scooped food onto his plate, patting his shoulder and keeping up a steady stream of conversation despite him speaking barely two words.

When she sent Quin into the kitchen for the second round of snickerdoodles, I turned my attention to Thurl. One ear flicked back and forth as he listened to his brothers, while the other stayed cocked in my direction. Even though he seemed fully present in the wider conversation, I felt he was aware of every twitch I made.

It was thrilling. I'd never had a man's undivided attention. Even boyfriends never seemed to be solely focused on me. They always had something that took precedence. Hockey for one, chess for another, and even a stupid television show for a third. It didn't matter what I needed. If it conflicted with their thing, then I was on my own.

It was nice to have someone who picked me for a change.

I shook my head at myself. I barely knew Thurl. He could be secretly obsessed with making dollhouses for all I knew. There was always a honeymoon period where I got dragged into the relationship with fake words and insincere acts of devotion.

I couldn't see Thurl making me go to a school event solo because a chess tournament was on TV. Well, I couldn't see Thurl going to a school event, to be fair, but not because he wouldn't want to.

"Why don't humans know about you?" I looked up to catch him with a half-eaten cookie on the way to his mouth. His hand reversed course before he answered.

"Society goes to great lengths to keep supernaturals hidden from humans."

"What does that mean? What happens to me now that I know?"

His hand tightened where it rested on my thigh. "Nothing. As long as you don't write a book about Society or in some other way attempt to expose us to the greater populace, nothing will happen to you."

"Keep the secret and it's fine?"

His head tilted to the side. "For some."

"How did I get a hall pass?"

The full force of his eyes pinned me to my chair. "Me. I'm your hall pass."

TWENTY-TWO

I WATCHED JADE carefully to make sure she was okay with my brothers and their sometimes raucous behavior (especially Quin's). She relaxed more and more as time passed, making my chest hurt with joy.

It evaporated when she asked me how she would fit into Society. I held my breath, waiting for her reaction.

"You mean, because I'm your mate?"

I tilted my muzzle in a curt nod.

She took a deep breath. "What if that doesn't work out?"

The cramp in my chest spread to my belly, and I abandoned the rest of the cookie on my plate. "Nothing will happen to you as long as I or my brothers live."

Her eyes widened and she scanned the table before her attention returned to me. "Your brothers would protect me? Why?"

"Because you are precious to me, and they are my brothers."

I didn't fully understand the question. They would protect her if I weren't able to do it. We were brothers. Raised as one and forged by our experiences. I would give my life for my family, which now included Kendal and Jade.

"You are our family. We protect what's ours." I winced, not wanting her to take that the wrong way. "Not that you belong to me."

She nodded, but stared at the wall without seeing for several long moments. "I've never experienced that level of loyalty." Her eyes darted to mine. "Of love. Other than with Nanna."

"Surely your mother loved you."

She huffed. "My mother had me because it was the expected thing to do among her friends. Go to college, get married, have babies. Only, after she had me, she realized she didn't actually want kids. Or a husband. They divorced, dad remarried and has a whole new family, and mom moved me in with Nanna so she could travel the world and be a nomad."

"I'm sorry." I never had a mother—or a father, for that matter. We had test tubes and incubators. Even so, I knew it must have hurt to grow up without parents when you had them.

"Don't be. Nanna more than made up for her. Besides, I was just a baby when she left and have only seen her a few times since then. Nanna's my mom, for all intents and purposes."

I nodded, dragged her chair closer, and tucked her under my arm. I couldn't imagine anyone not wanting her. I wanted her with every cell in my body. I desired her, yes, but it was more than that. I wanted to make her smile every day, provide her with everything she could ever want, revel in her slightest touch.

In so short a time, she had become my everything.

Drym and Kendal said their goodbyes first, with her giggling out the door. The rest filed out after them. Nanna stopped Roul from leaving and hugged Jade.

"I'm going to stay with Roul."

Jade's eyes shot to mine and I looked at Roul. I didn't think any of us could deny the old woman anything, but I worried about her disrupting his moody isolation.

He grunted. "It's fine."

I nodded at Jade to reassure her before she turned back to her grandmother.

"You be back first thing in the morning. And for heaven's sake, don't assault him."

"I think he can defend himself, dear." Nanna patted Jade's arm.

Jade glared at her. "That's not the assault I'm worried about."

Nanna laughed and waved us both off as Roul helped her down the steps. She stopped several steps from the woods to turn back and shout at Jade, "Do all the things I would do!" Then she nearly lost her balance as she cackled. The largest of us, Roul was stooped over, allowing Nanna to use his forearm as a cane as they continued their slow shuffle toward his house.

Jade shook her head. "I hope he knows what he's in for."

I cocked my head at their retreating forms. "Of all of us, he's the one who needs her the most. Maybe she can bring him out of the darkness he's embraced."

"That sounds ominous. He's not dangerous, is he?"

I looked down to catch Jade worrying her bottom lip with her teeth. "No. The woman we believe to be his mate—the same witch who helped us escape—stayed behind with BioSynth, the lab that created us."

Jade gasped. "That's awful. Why would she do such a thing?"

"She wants to help take them down once and for all, probably not realizing the pain Roul is in without her."

"And there's no way to contact her and let her know? It's noble for her to want to help, but it's not fair what it's doing to him."

Her eyes went wide and her hand flew to her mouth. "What if she rejects him as her mate? Would he feel better then?"

I didn't want to answer her. If I told her the truth, then it might sway her to make a decision she wouldn't ordinarily choose. But I couldn't lie to her.

"Can I not answer that question until our relationship is resolved?"

A tiny, "Oh," escaped her lips before they pressed into a thin line and she nodded.

I grinned and changed the subject, grateful she let me. "I think Nanna left enough snickerdoodles to feed an army."

It took a few beats, but she smiled back. "Or a pack of wyrfangs."

"That's true." We ate more than half of what she'd made. I wasn't sure if the sweet tooth we shared came from our dragon or werewolf DNA, but it was strong. Ever since Kendal introduced us to the wonder that is cupcakes, we couldn't seem to get enough sugary treats.

Kendal often said it was a good thing our metabolisms worked overtime.

"What can we do to thank her for cooking for us?" It would be a pittance for how grateful I felt for her raising Jade. Caring for her. Giving her a home.

She spun and looked at me, horrified. "Oh, absolutely not! You'll do nothing. She would be offended at the very idea. Like I said, she sees feeding people as an important task and it's up to her to make sure no one in her vicinity goes hungry. Why do you think I look like this?"

She waved a hand up and down her body and I couldn't help but follow the movement with my eyes. I traced her curves, lingering on the bit of skin showing above her collar.

"I would drape her in jewels for that alone."

Jade's laugh sputtered as she looked at me, my desire naked on my face for her to see. I knew my eyes blazed with the heat that coursed through my veins. I slowly reached out and traced a finger down her cheek. She closed her eyes and leaned in to my touch.

Her lips parted and her breath came faster as I slid my fingers through her hair to cup the back of her head and neck. I locked my muscles. I wanted nothing more than to gather her in my arms and carry her into the house. Lay her down on the first soft surface and bury my head between her thighs.

Her arousal coated the air and I no longer cared if she was only curious. I would take whatever scraps I could get.

Her eyes blinked open and the heat I saw reflected there almost took me to my knees.

"Please," she whispered.

"Please what? What do you need from me? Ask, and I would give you the world."

TWENTY-THREE

I HAD NO idea what I asked him for. I just knew I needed something from him.

Nope, I'm a liar. I knew exactly what I wanted from him, but I didn't know if I dared go there. Could I go there? Mentally I was pretty sure all of my lady bits enthusiastically said yes. Physically, I wasn't sure.

But then, surely Kendal made it work somehow with Drym. It had to be physically possible, right?

Was I brave enough to find out? That wasn't the right question. The right question was, how badly would I hate myself if I didn't give it the old college try?

I stared at Thurl, who patiently waited for an answer, his body still and his eyes locked on mine, blazing red like some unholy demon who wanted to consume me.

And oh boy, did I want to be consumed.

"You. I want you."

"What do you want from me, Jade?"

"I want you to make love to me."

The words were out before I could overthink them, and I nearly sagged in relief when he scooped me into his arms and carried me inside. He didn't bother to shut the door. I smiled as I thought that whoever was stupid enough to trespass on the 'fangs' territory wouldn't make it near the houses, much less inside.

That was my last coherent thought.

Thurl set me on my feet next to his massive bed. His claws started a slow descent down my sides. They stopped just above my waistband.

"I will stop at any point as soon as you say the word."

His growl raised goosebumps and made me squeeze my thighs together. I could no more speak than fly, so I nodded.

I squeaked as he shoved his cold nose into my neck, but a warm huff followed it. Then his tongue flicked out and licked above my collar. I answered his hum with a moan. He slipped his claws into the waistband of my jeans.

"Off."

I fumbled with the button, only to be met with the Sisyphean task of lowering the zipper. The silicone covered tips of his claws drew patterns on my sides and back and I had the concentration of a squirrel on meth.

I ended up just yanking the two halves apart; the zipper falling on its own. I shoved my pants over the swell of my ass and they dropped to my ankles. I went to step out of them and almost fell on my ass, having completely forgotten about my shoes.

Luckily, Thurl's reflexes were faster than gravity. His brows furrowed in concern before he smiled as I cracked up. Only I could turn a sexy moment into utter disaster. "Um, shoes. Gotta take my shoes off first." I twisted and sat on the bed, still snickering as I undid the laces and kicked them and my pants off. When I stood up, his giant hand spanned my chest and pushed, sending me flat on my back.

For a second, my brain blanked. His bed was so soft, the blankets already singing their siren call, urging me to climb further in.

And then Thurl dragged my panties down my thighs, and his tongue speared between my folds. After that, all my thoughts were two boxes of Scrabble tiles gleefully thrown to the floor by a toddler. A split second of self-consciousness at being naked and splayed in front of him was drowned out as my entire body lit up like a runway.

He'd pushed his shoulders between my thighs, spreading me wide open, but then he placed my feet on his shoulders and ate my pussy like it was his job and he was up for a promotion. Jesus, I was going to make him the CEO. My thigh muscles clenched, and my back arched off the bed as he cosplay'd Blackbeard and plundered my treasure.

When he flicked his tongue inside me and his tiny front teeth rubbed across my clit, I came like a freight train. Literally. My thighs clickity-clacked like train wheels on a track and the noises I made may as well have been an air whistle. I warned the entire compound of my approach.

He continued to lick and nibble my thighs as I floated back to earth. Not many of the men I'd been with had gone down on me, and none of them had done it like *that*. They seemed to get bored long before I was near ready to orgasm and stuck it in to get themselves off.

I was still panting when I deemed my lungs well enough to speak. "You didn't have to do that."

My belly quivered as he nipped above my belly button.

"Yes, I did. Your scent was driving me mad. I had to taste you." His hands skimmed up my sides, and then he loomed over me. "You're delicious."

I should probably be mortified, but my body punched my ticket, found my seat, and was ready for the ride.

"Are you okay?"

I sighed happily. "Never been more okay in my life."

I felt the blunt tip of his penis push against my entrance and I sat straight up, pushed on his chest until he stepped back and gawked. "I'm, uh… not sure that thing is going to fit."

His nose tipped down and then his whole body crouched as he inspected my vagina. Then, I was mortified.

"I might be slightly larger than the others…"

I squeaked and my face flamed. Were we really having this conversation?

"But Drym assures me a human female's channel is flexible and that Kendal has no trouble taking him."

I suppose we were.

He looked out the bedroom door before turning back to me. "I can call her if you'd like to talk with her about it."

I flung my hand over my eyes. "No. No, I really don't want to discuss your and Drym's penises, thanks."

"You're welcome."

I guessed the 'fangs were still learning about sarcasm. I reached out and touched him, feeling the stiff but flexible spikes between my fingers again. His eyes closed and he groaned. I felt a heady rush of power that I could affect him like that. This huge, deadly monster melted like fine chocolate under my touch. A new rush of desire flowed through me. "Just go really slow, okay?"

He bobbed his head fast enough to send his ears flopping. He crawled over me again, forcing me onto my back. His arms caged me in, his huge hands on either side of my head as his knee came between my legs, spreading me impossibly wide. "I would not be the cause of any pain, Jade. I will stop the instant I think you're hurt."

I decided explaining that a little pain would be okay since it adds to the pleasure wouldn't be wise at the moment, so I just nodded.

And he pushed.

The wyrfangs didn't have pupils, but I could always tell where his focus was somehow. The intense scrutiny I was under as he eased himself into me unlocked a new kink. My hands flew to his sides, fingers buried in his fur as my back arched, urging him closer.

Time was agonizing as he stopped after every inch, his gaze never leaving mine as he gauged my reactions. I moaned at the delicious scrape of those spikes against my walls and gasped when he hit my g-spot just right. I'd started thinking I didn't have one. Nobody else had ever found it, including me. But the rush of heat, the clench of my muscles and my throbbing clit screamed *yes!* like we'd summited Everest.

He stopped and I whimpered. He must have thought it was in pain because he started to pull back out. I clamped my heels on his back and practically growled, "Do. Not. Stop."

His answering growl vibrated my chest and lit every one of the ten thousand, two-hundred and eighty nerves in my clit into a raging inferno. I think my eyes rolled back in my head when he bottomed out. Something kind of hard, like a marble beneath his skin, hit my clit and I exploded. *Choo Choo.*

He still studied me when my vision cleared.

"Are you okay?"

"I think I finally understand why the French call it 'the little death.' I've died. This is heaven, and I'm never leaving."

He chuckled and then we both groaned as he pulled partway out, causing a pussy aftershock to clamp down on him. He slid back in, and as he started getting into a rhythm, I would have sworn there was such a thing as too much pleasure. Too many orgasms were going to turn me blind or make a pumpkin grow in my stomach. Or was that a watermelon?

I sucked in a breath. "Stop, stop!"

"Have I hurt you?"

"No. We just forgot something very important. Can you get me pregnant? And what about diseases? I know I'm clean because I was practically a born-again virgin, but what about you?"

His answer rushed out as he pushed back inside. "Cavi doesn't think we can get you pregnant, and I was engineered to be insusceptible to all disease. I cannot get sick, and you cannot get me sick."

"Okay, good. That's good." His speed was increasing and my brain was ceasing to work. My body reduced to a single point, focused on what was happening in and around my pussy. Every time he pushed in, that hard marble—gods bless it, whatever it was—hit my clit and my g-spot was pulsing like his cock started a rave.

It didn't take long before my back surged up in my fourth or fifth orgasm of the night. Who was counting? After that, his hips pistoned into me at warp speed, and either I had one two-minute orgasm or they ran together so close I couldn't tell where one ended and the next began. His cum triggered the grand finale and, like the end of a fireworks show, it left me panting and exhausted.

I was going to be so sore the next day. That was a problem for future me. Present me was gathered in his arms as he rolled over, then positioned on his chest. I caught my breath as his silicone-covered claws gently ran up and down my back. I fell asleep with sticky thighs, too worn out to get up and take a shower.

TWENTY-FOUR

MY MATE WAS perfect in every way. Her soft snores ruffled the fur on my shoulder and her small hands buried in my sides. The love I felt for her was all-consuming. The need to bite her, to cement the bond, was now a hyper fixation.

I knew from Drym and Kendal that our mating bond allowed us to feel when our mate felt pain, but more importantly, it manifested as a rope of dancing lights that tied us together. I could always find her, always know if she was hurt.

The need for that level of connection to her demanded I bite her as soon as possible. But I wouldn't do so without her consent. And if she rejected me? I was positive I would end up a shell. Maybe even dangerous to those around me, lost in the fog that overtook our reasoning when we were pushed too far.

The sky was light purple when she finally stirred. She sat up, her eyes squinted and blinking. I had removed her glasses as she slept, afraid they would be lost or broken. I held them to her chest and she slid them on, patting at her hair.

"Do I look thoroughly fucked? Because I feel thoroughly fucked."

I chuckled and my cock rubbed between her legs. She slid off me and crossed her ankles. "Nope. Too soon. Too much stimulation. I'm going to find my thickest granny panties and put thick leggings on over those. I don't think I could handle the barest brush of a seam right now."

My muzzle hit my chest. "I am sorry."

Her eyes lit up and she laughed. "I'm not complaining. Just saying I'm not going to be up for round two anytime soon."

I grinned. "I am patient."

She looked at me from the corner of her eyes. "I bet."

She grabbed my hand and led me into the bathroom, stepping in the oversized shower and turning the water on. I shuddered and pulled against her hold.

Her brows crinkled as she looked up at me. "What's wrong?"

I licked at my muzzle. "I don't like water."

She looked back at the shower, then at my seam. My fur was matted from our activity and our combined cum which had run down the inside of my thighs while she slept.

"Is it the water, or the sensation of the water falling on you?"

"A bit of both, but more the sensation." If I wanted her to be my mate, I needed to start opening up about our experience in the lab. "They didn't allow us to bathe. Instead, they dropped soap flakes on us and sprayed us with high-powered hoses."

Her fingers clenched on my forearm before she wrapped me in a hug. I hung on until she looked up at me. Her eyes swung to the massive tub. She stepped out of my hold and turned the shower off. The tub filled as she tested the temperature with her hand. "Let's try this instead. I won't fill it much, just enough to wet and rinse ourselves."

She took my hands in each of hers. "You are in control. Take as much time as you need getting in, and get out if you get uncomfortable. I'll wait for you."

She dropped my hands and stepped backward into the tub, sinking in the few inches of water. Drym wasn't shy about sharing how pleasurable he found water now, but the fear was well entrenched in me.

Jade didn't watch me or try to get me to join her. She sat and bathed herself. The washcloth ran over her skin in a caress I wished was mine. Wanting it to be my hands soaping her body pushed me over the rim of the tub.

The water was warm, and Jade didn't make a big deal of me being in it. She handed me a second washcloth, and I quickly scrubbed my lower half before holding it out in a silent plea.

"Do you want me to wash you?"

I shook my head. "No, I want to wash you. Is that okay?"

She grinned and spun and rested her back against my chest. I started slowly rubbing the cloth over her body, marveling at the feel of her skin beneath my palms.

By the time she shivered from the water going cold, I'd forgotten where we were.

I'd have to tell Drym he was right. Being in water could be quite nice.

We dried off with fluffy towels, and I eyed the bed with longing. I knew there wouldn't be a round two, as she said, for a while yet, but it didn't make me want her less. She was pulling on her panties—a blue pair dotted with tiny flowers which came up to her belly button and well down on her legs—when Nanna's voice carried upstairs.

"Yoo-hoo! Are y'all indecent?"

Jade rolled her eyes. "Partly. We'll be right down." She caught me staring at her perfect ass. "Why are you looking at me like that?"

"Because I want to eat you. I want to hear you scream my name again."

Her blush spread down her chest. "I screamed your name?"

"Several times."

She covered her face and shook her head. "I'm in the ugliest pair of underwear I own, my pussy feeling wrecked, and you still made me wet. Please behave. At least until I feel steady on my feet again."

I bowed my head to her. "I'll do my best."

Her eyes narrowed on me and I chuckled. She grew still and serious and my ears fell, my claws scratching at the fur on my thighs.

"We need to talk about the mate thing."

Ice ran through my veins. "Can we wait until later?" *Can I enjoy you for the day? Can I have you one more time before you tear me in two?*

She gave me a smile. "Yes, we can wait until later."

My elation came close to how I felt when we freed ourselves from BioSynth. I vowed to be present every minute I had left with her.

TWENTY-FIVE

IF IT WEREN'T for his ears, I might never know how Thurl was feeling. Very expressive, those pointed ears of his. When I mentioned talking about being his mate, they drooped like a two-week-old flower arrangement. They sprang back to attention when I said we could talk later.

He obviously thought I was going to reject him.

I wasn't sure. I needed more information, thus the talk. I certainly wasn't ready to give him up, but did I want to be permanently tied to him?

After my last boyfriend bust, I figured I'd be the single old cat lady of the neighborhood. I was fine with that. Mostly. The sex toys available these days were incredible, but Thurl was packing something even the most creative company hadn't thought up.

And he was so warm. And cozy. And I'm not ashamed to admit it was nice knowing he could keep me safe. Especially since being a witness and being attacked were probably connected. *Oh, you're a drug lord? How cute. Meet my monstrous boyfriend, who has teeth, claws, and horns and was bred to be a weapon.*

The only problem being that I couldn't stay here forever. I would need to go back to work, and I couldn't rely on Emma to take care of my clowder. Thurl seemed fine with the cats, but I guessed having a dozen instead of just two in his house would be a bit much.

If I had all the money in the world, I could quit teaching and work with Emma at the rescue. That was a pipe dream I liked to bring out and dust off on the weekends. I'd miss my kids, but the cats were my first love.

The smell of breakfast filled the kitchen. Nanna had covered every inch of counter space with bacon, sausage, eggs, pancakes, toast, and fruit. She hadn't been there long enough to make all of it, and I didn't think there was a crumb left in Thurl's pantry after the night before, so I must owe Roul a trip to the grocery store.

Metaphorically speaking, of course. I giggled at the thought of the massive, red-eyed beast choosing a cantaloupe in the produce section.

Said beast came through the front door, loaded down with even more platters of food.

"Just set those anywhere, dear, and bring in the rest."

My mouth fell open. "The rest? There's more?"

"Of course there is. None of the 'fangs know how to cook, and Kendal admitted she could burn water. With as huge as they are, they need a lot of calories."

She gave me an exaggerated wink and I braced myself.

"Besides, if you two got up to what I would've gotten up to last night, you need the nourishment."

I groaned and rolled my eyes.

Thurl leaned down and whispered in my ear, "She's not wrong."

I sent my elbow backwards into his belly. "Don't encourage her."

Nanna sighed and threw the back of her hand up to her forehead. "Alas, I couldn't tempt any of the unattached, even after I gave them a rundown on my affair with Killian. Young people these days just don't appreciate the experience that comes with age."

Roul reappeared carrying what I hoped was the last of the trays. I reached out and grabbed his forearm.

"Did she assault you?"

He grunted.

"I'm sorry, I don't speak grunts. I can go grab a doll and you can point to where the bad touches happened."

His lips twitched up in the weakest excuse for a smile I'd ever seen. It was glorious. I decided in that second that cheering him up was my new mission in life. I added a mental note to talk to Thurl about finding his mate while we talked tonight.

I was sure she had no idea how it was affecting him for her to be gone. If only she knew, she would come back.

Unless she planned to reject him.

I frowned. That was no good. No, I couldn't think that way. She just didn't know, and I was determined for her to find out.

Thurl waited until Roul unburdened himself before asking, "The others?"

"On their way."

Nanna patted his elbow. I'm sure she meant the pat for his shoulder, but she was too short to reach.

"Go sit down now." She followed him with her eyes, a small smile on her lips. "Such a good boy."

I choked. "Nanna! They aren't dogs."

She waggled her eyebrows. "Oh, I'm well aware. I just mean that he's incredibly sweet and kind."

It was Thurl's turn to choke. He left my side and went to sit next to Roul, where they exchanged a flurry of whispers. I made my way to Nanna.

"Are you okay?"

She beamed up at me. "I'm perfectly fine. He's so sweet. Every time I got up to go pee, he would check on me. Make sure I didn't need anything." She took a deep breath. "I don't know what's made him so sad, but I'd like to give her a swift kick in the canoe."

I laughed. "How do you know it's a her?"

"Honey, that kind of sad is always heartbreak."

The arrival of Quin raised the volume in the house and made side conversations impossible. When the three humans were patting the food babies in their bellies and the 'fangs were polishing off every scrap of the food, Kendal came to check on me.

"Settling in okay?"

"Yes, I have. I don't know where you found that mattress, but it's heaven." I felt the blush creep up my neck and hoped she would ignore it.

"I'm glad you enjoyed it." She didn't wink, but it was clear in her voice.

I had to laugh. If there was anyone else in the entire world who knew what the experience was like, it was her. Which brought to mind… "Can you tell me about the mate thing?"

"Sure. What do you want to know?"

"Everything. All Thurl has said is that it's permanent, but it's my decision. He implied that he'd be more than heartbroken if I reject him."

Her voice went up an octave. "Are you going to reject him?"

"I don't think so. I don't know. I need more information. I don't think I can decide without knowing everything." I stared out the window, which was the only place I could avoid anyone looking back. "How did you decide?"

Kendal snorted. "Drym and I sort of bonded through trauma. I was drawn to him instantly and fell completely in love. There was… a lot going on, and I wanted that connection. The decision was simple for me." She leaned forward to catch my eyes. "I get that it's difficult, but sometimes the leap is worth it. What does your gut say?"

I looked at Thurl. He was crouched next to Nanna's chair, his palms out as she piled cookies into his hands. The way he'd folded his body looked uncomfortable. My gut said he would sit there for as long as she wanted him to. He was big and objectively scary looking. His claws and teeth were sharp. He could probably stab people with his horns, and I was pretty sure my attacker was no longer living or in one piece.

But he was a marshmallow. Soft and squishy on the inside. I wanted to take care of him.

Holy crap. I wanted to love him.

I spent the rest of what turned into brunch in a daze. I'm not sure I responded appropriately when spoken to, or even at all. I vaguely remembered being asked direct questions. I was lost in my head, analyzing my feelings from every angle I could.

Would it be so bad to mate with Thurl? What was the worst possible outcome? That we grew to hate each other? That happened to married couples all the time. Even without the remedy of divorce, I'm sure some kind of mutually beneficial solution could be found.

He'd said 'fated mate.'

Meant for each other. In a designed way, not an amorphous one. Specifically created or chosen for each other.

Why would the fates choose to pair mates who'd grow to resent each other?

They wouldn't.

Taking that off the table, the worst possible outcome was us—what? Growing old together? Living happily ever after?

I was delusional. Seeing an outcome I wanted to see. Rose-colored glasses shoved firmly up my nose. There had to be a catch.

I barely registered when Thurl took my hand and led me outside and pushed me into the porch swing. He crouched in front of me, his ears at half-mast.

"Are you all right?"

I nodded. Tried for a smile but it fizzled. "I'm fine."

His tongue licked at his muzzle as he inspected the porch boards. "Would you like to talk now?"

His entire frame sagged like an old balloon. I stomped the urge to run my fingers through the fur at his neck and stiffened my spine. "What's the catch?"

His head tilted, but that porch board was fascinating. "Catch?"

"There has to be a catch, right? Nothing is ever perfect. Why should the mate thing be any different?"

The back door swung open with a bang and we both jumped. Nanna smiled softly at me, her hands wrapped around a thick binder held to her chest. She stepped around Thurl and held it out to me.

"I borrowed this from the common hall. I knew you'd be analyzing every angle, but sweetheart, some things can't be analyzed. Magic, the fates, and most of the supernatural world fall into that category."

I took the binder from her and stared down at its nondescript cover.

"That said," she waved her hand at the book, "they can be explained a bit better than a wave of the hand and a mumbled abracadabra."

She patted Thurl on the head. "Come help an old woman clean up. Jade will be in after a while."

I caught his worried look from the corner of my eye before he followed Nanna inside. My focus was on the table of contents which identified this binder as about shifters. Highlighted in the table of contents was "The Fates & Fated Mates." I thumbed through to that section and read.

Thirty minutes later, I flipped back to the table of contents. There was a phone number, preceded by the word "bacon." I hoped I wasn't about to call a butcher, but I had one question left and if the person on the other end of this line could answer it, then I'd risk buying some breakfast meat.

I barely heard a single ring before a lilting female voice answered.

"Go for Bacon."

"Umm… hi."

"Hi?" She drew the word out, making it even more of a question.

"Sorry." I cleared my throat and started over. "I'm Jade, and I'm holding a binder that you gave to … a friend of mine. I have a question and saw this number on the table of contents page."

"Oh. Well then, hello Jade. What can I do for you?"

I had no idea if the person on the other end of the line knew about Society, or the wyrfangs in particular. Her number was in the book, but people changed numbers all the time. "Do you know my friend?"

"If you're holding the binder, then yes, we've met. Which one of the 'fangs is your friend?"

I let out a sigh of relief. "Thurl."

"Oooh, red eyes, big arms. So, what can I do for you, Jade?"

"Are the fates ever wrong?"

"What?"

"Do they ever get it wrong? Are there fated mates who end up not standing each other and being miserable?"

I heard her chuckle. "Those bitches have a one-hundred-percent perfect track record. It's why all the shifters were so heartbroken when they were cut off from mates—though they seemed to have reversed course on that."

"Your binder explained that. They were mad at Fenrir?"

"Yeah, the ultimate player and dead set on bagging a moirae. Idiot. Now mates are popping up all over, relatively speaking. Well, at least in Damruck."

Silence reigned for several moments before she cleared her throat.

"Look, Jade, I know it's scary, especially for someone new to Society, but if Thurl is your mate, you have nothing to worry about."

"He says I am, but how do *I* know?"

"As long as I've known them, which I admit isn't long, none of the 'fangs have lied. Even about the smallest thing. The type of trauma they lived through forges a person. You come out the other side either good or evil, and they're good ones."

I chewed my bottom lip. "You sound like you're talking from personal experience."

"I am."

She didn't elaborate. My heart ached for her, but I didn't press. "Then I suppose I only have one more question."

"Shoot."

"Why Bacon?"

She snort laughed, which set off my own giggles.

TWENTY-SIX

MY EARS FLICKED as they picked up Jade talking. I leaned toward the back door like it would help me hear better. As if I couldn't hear everything she said standing upright.

Nanna appeared in front of me and slapped my bicep. I rubbed at it automatically, shrinking back from the old woman.

"Don't eavesdrop. She'll tell you if she wants you to know."

"Yes, ma'am."

Her tiny fingers grabbed my wrist in a grip stronger than expected. She tugged, and I allowed her to lead me toward the front of the house. I could still hear Jade speaking, and if I focused, I could hear what she said.

Nanna pinched me. "Stop listening in!"

I drooped. "I can't help it. She's my focus."

"You love her."

My eyes flicked to hers. "She's my mate."

The older woman grabbed my muzzle and shook it. "That's not what I said."

My words garbled as they pushed through my trapped mouth. "Yes, I love her."

Nanna nodded and released me. She sank into an armchair. Sized for me and my brothers, it swallowed her.

"Good, but she'll need time. Just because she's a kindergarten teacher doesn't mean she easily swallows a bunch of mystical woo woo. She needs to come to her own conclusion about being your mate."

I nodded. "Of course."

Jade's screech of "What?" had both of us running for the back door. My claws flexed, and my lips pulled into a snarl as I scanned the backyard for threats. There were none. I turned toward Jade, who now clutched Nanna's hand in her own, her eyes wide as she stared at nothing.

The man on the other end of the phone was telling her about an incident at her house. Her friend Emma had been attacked while feeding Jade's cats.

I recognized his voice. He was the older detective who'd been at her house. He was trying to convince her to return to police protection. My chest rumbled and I shook my head.

She was safer with me.

"I appreciate your concern, Detective Chambers, but I assure you, I am safer right where I am."

The man sighed, but relented, and Jade ended the call.

"Is she okay?" Nanna's voice didn't tremble, but her upset was clear to my senses.

As was Jade's fear. Outwardly, she was calm and collected. But her heart raced, her breaths were shallow, and the scent of fear was strong.

"She's shaken, her neck is sore, and she has a small cut on her neck. Apparently, they were waiting in the house. They grabbed her hair as she passed the kitchen door and yanked her head back. Put a knife to her throat, but stopped when they saw it wasn't me. Then they ran off."

She looked up at me.

"They want me to go into police custody."

I shook my head again. My throat closed up at the idea of her not being with me. My hands fisted at my sides, claws cutting through their caps and into my palms.

She nodded. "I told them no. I feel safer with you." She turned to Nanna. "I want you to stay here, too. It's not a leap for them to go after you to get to me."

"What about my friends at Sunset Springs?"

"I think that's one degree of separation too many. They should be fine, but call them and tell them to be extra cautious."

Nanna nodded and scurried back inside. I stepped forward, wrapping Jade in my arms. She sagged against me.

"I got my friend hurt."

My teeth ground together. "No. Your attackers hurt your friend."

She took a deep breath and let it out slowly, her breath warming my chest. "I want to go see her." She pulled away and looked up at me. "And I need to figure out what to do about my cats."

"Bring them here. I'll get my brothers to help so we can get them all in one trip."

Her mouth fell open. "You'd … you'd do that for me?"

I ran the back of my finger over her soft cheek. "I would do anything for you."

She swallowed and we stood, stared into each other's eyes, and the minutes ticked by. She shook her head and straightened her spine. Took a step back, and nodded.

I wasn't sure what decision she'd made, but she seemed determined.

"Okay then. Let's do it. We'll need to hurry so we can get it done before dawn."

It wasn't hard to marshal my brothers. Even Kendal came, as an extra pair of hands. We made the trip to Jade's house in good time. Once there, we showed her our military precision and obedience. She pointed and commanded. We did as she said. In short order, we had the cats in carriers, their food, dishes, and litter boxes packed. Kendal scooped as many toys as she could find into a bag. Quin put giant bags of litter on each shoulder. The rest of us grabbed two carriers a piece, and within forty-five minutes, we were on our way back to the compound.

Most of the cats were silent. The smallest of them, a kitten Jade said she'd adopted only a few weeks ago, screamed like it was being tortured. We winced every time the small ball of fur let out its meow. They seemed to rise in volume and duration.

It was the first one set free inside my house.

"Sorry about Cameow. She hasn't fully adjusted and still thinks she's going to starve if she doesn't remind me of her presence. Loudly. And often." Jade winced.

My brothers assured her it was fine and then beat hasty retreats. I watched as Jade set up the cat's supplies around my house. Two water fountains and a bowl sat along one kitchen wall, twelve matching food bowls along another. She distributed litterboxes around the entire house, with cats following behind, eager to christen each one as soon as it was done.

I also followed as she moved through her tasks, not wanting to leave her for even a second. This crime organization was getting bolder. They didn't know where she was, I was certain of that, but my nerves were on high alert.

"It's very nice of you to house my cats like this. I know they're a lot."

She was turned away from me, stroking the back of a solid white cat. Her head was bent and she looked tiny and tired in that moment.

"I enjoy having them here."

She jerked her eyes to mine, disbelief clear on her face.

"It's true. They soothe you and make you happy. I welcome into my home anything that will make you feel…" Like it's your home. Like it's where you belong. Like it's where you want to stay. With me. "Better," I finished lamely.

It was true. I liked seeing her things here. I wanted her so deeply entrenched in my house, my life, my heart that she'd find it impossible to dig her way out. I wanted her to take ownership of all that I was.

I would never say it. I wanted her to choose me—not under pressure or because of anything I said—but because she wanted me.

"Thurl," she whispered, "I want to bond with you."

My immediate reaction was elation, followed by recoil. I shook my head even as my eyes blazed brighter. "It's too soon."

"It *is* soon, you're right." She inhaled sharply. "But I spoke to Bacon. I read the binder. Everything says the fates don't make mistakes."

I started to argue but she cut me off.

"I want you to bite me. I feel it, too, you know."

My mouth watered and I locked my muscles to keep from falling on her, tearing her clothes off and sinking my fangs into the soft flesh of her thigh. My voice was low and strained. "Are you sure?"

She met my eyes with her own and nodded. "Yes."

"Thank fuck."

TWENTY-SEVEN

HE WAS LIKE a taut rope, pulled past its limits and snapped. My words released him from whatever cage he'd put himself in and Thurl scooped me off the floor. Pawssonova hissed at the rough treatment and launched from my lap with a disgruntled look.

I would have shrugged, but Thurl's warm body trapped me. Before I could fully form a thought, I was on our bed—when had I started thinking of this bed as ours?—stripped of my pants and my monster's hands wrapped around my thighs, spreading me wide with a delicious pinch of his claws.

His breath hitched as he hovered over my hips, his gaze flicking down my body with an intensity that made me squirm. My pulse quickened, a drumbeat echoing in my ears, and I could practically taste the heat rising from him. Each growl sent shivers cascading over my skin, igniting a fire deep within me.

"This is what you want?" His voice was gravelly and unsure, velvet against the tension in the room. The vulnerability that lay beneath his fierce strength mesmerized me. "Once we bond, there's no backing out."

I held his gaze. I understood the implications. This meant forever. "I know," I breathed back, my heart racing as I laid my hands on the sides of his face, my thumbs brushed over his cheekbones, his fur warm beneath my fingers. "I read the information in the binder. I understand, but more than that, I can feel it. It's what I want, Thurl."

His jaw clenched, and the friction of my fingers against him spun the response into a singular shared moment. A suspended breath caught between us. Then he leaned closer, pressing his nose between my legs, his deep inhale sending cool air over my heated flesh. It felt as if the world outside—and all the dangers that lurked within it—faded.

"If you're sure," he murmured, eyes like molten lava, burning with intensity.

I rolled my eyes. "Yes, I'm sure. Now bite me before I'm so frustrated I scream."

He looked up at me and his eyes blazed. He was pure beast in that moment. There was nothing tamed about him, and I marveled at the power I held over him. This monster would—had—killed for me. I knew in that moment there was nothing he wouldn't do to keep me safe.

His jaw dropped open, and I braced for the sharp sting of his teeth, but his tongue darted out and traced lazily up my inner thigh. He gave my other leg the same maddening treatment before finally swiping his tongue through the folds of my pussy.

I moaned in relief. Each flick of his wicked, forked tongue ignited my skin and sent shock waves deep into my core. A primal, desperate need that clawed for release.

Thurl growled against me. My head fell back, my hands fisted in the sheets at my sides, my thighs trembled as he licked and sucked at my clit. I forgot all about the impending bite, my thoughts centered on how he played my body like a Stradivarius.

"You are so beautiful."

My knee jerk scoff stuck in my throat when he nibbled at my soft folds. The way he played my body made me almost believe.

With every curl of his forked tongue as it dipped inside, only to return to my clit like a long-lost friend, he coaxed me higher, closer to ecstasy. The world outside faded. My entire focus on the feel of Thurl's tongue, his hot breath, the small sting of his claws where they held my thighs open.

My core fluttered, and my back bowed off the bed. I fell over the edge, swallowed by the most intense orgasm of my life. Sparks flared behind my closed eyelids as wave after wave of unimaginable pleasure flowed over and through me. It was so intense I thought I might die.

Happily, I might add.

I barely felt Thurl's teeth sink into the crease of flesh at my upper thigh. His upper jaw piercing a line to my hipbone, his lower in the crease of my butt cheek.

The prick set off another wave, stronger than the ones before. My body quaked as pleasure tightened my muscles and unwound my brain. I surrendered to the bliss, to his hold, to him.

"Thurl," I gasped, not sure what I asked for but needing something to ground me before I shattered and my dust floated into the stars. I grasped his horns and tugged with all my strength, which equaled that of a moth, but he indulged me.

He rose over me, his eyes impossibly bright.

No, it wasn't entirely his eyes. There were now motes of red light dancing around us, a halo that bobbed and weaved as we breathed.

I inhaled. "What?"

Thurl's head tilted as he studied the tiny balls of light. "Our bond." His eyes met mine as his cock slid home.

You'd think after the never-ending orgasm I'd just had, I'd need time to recover before another, but when he moved, that coil in my belly wrapped tighter and threatened to spring loose in seconds.

The spikes on the sides of his dick swirled in and out of me and hit all the right spots. His heat wrapped me like a furnace, and the balls of light—our bond—pulsed in time with his thrusts, giving the room a disco effect.

I felt like I was on the verge of an aneurysm. And I wasn't even sure what an aneurysm was.

My voice cried out, "More… harder…" and I had no idea where it came from, but Thurl obliged with a low, grunting growl that raised goosebumps on my skin. Nothing had ever felt more right in my life and I wanted to fuse myself to him. I would have chuckled at the thought if I hadn't orgasmed the orgasm to end all orgasms.

I think I blacked out.

Thurl stared down at me. "Are you all right?"

"I have no idea."

He scanned my body as if he tried to determine for me. I chuckled, then dissolved into a full belly laugh. When I sobered,

I cupped his muzzle and kissed his cold nose. "Yes. I'm fine. I feel like a sponge that a compactor squeezed, but I'm fine."

I reached up to bat at one of the dancing lights. It drifted on the breeze I'd created before settling back into line with the others. "This is our bond?"

Thurl nodded. "Drym and Kendal described it as a tether of balls of light."

"A tether?" Visions of only being able to go so far from Thurl before being violently yanked back filled my head.

"Of sorts. It's non-corporeal, and it will stretch between us no matter how far or wide we roam from each other." He glanced away. "I will feel your pain as well."

"Like, literally? If I get a papercut, you'll feel it?"

He nodded. "On the very same finger."

"What about you? If you're hurt, will I feel it?"

"We assume it works both ways."

I sat up, my scientific curiosity overwhelming any other thought I might have. "Let's test it. Scratch your arm."

He shook his head. "No. I will not have you feel pain."

"But I'm curious. I want to know."

He shook his head again.

I *humphed.* "Fine." As quick as I could, I pinched his chest. My brows slashed down. "I didn't feel anything."

The corner of his mouth tilted in a smirk. "I'm not sure you would, since that didn't hurt."

I smacked his bicep. "Come on, just one small scratch on your arm and we'll know if it works both ways."

He shook his head and I squealed in frustration. "It's going to drive me crazy not knowing, and thus I will drive you crazy."

His muzzle tipped to the ceiling. In thought or exasperation, I wasn't sure, but I knew I was close to winning.

"It doesn't have to be deep or long. Just enough for you to feel it."

He grunted and used his thumb to pop the cap off his index claw. After a deep breath, he pushed it past his fur and into the skin of his forearm.

I stared at my arm with bated breath. The sting came without preamble. I rubbed at the spot. "Okay, yeah. I felt that."

Thurl fussed like it was me that was bleeding.

My stomach twisted at the pain. Not what I'd felt, but what I'd caused him. "Okay, we're never doing that again."

TWENTY-EIGHT

WITH JADE'S EXPERIMENT concluded to her satisfaction (not mine—knowing she felt any pain sent a spike through my heart), she fell fast asleep. I watched over her. I wanted to crawl into bed with her, snuggle up and wrap her in my arms, but I was restless. Unable to settle in one place for long.

My fur itched. Even though I sensed no danger, my mind was on high alert. Something triggered my protective instincts, but I couldn't work out where the threat lay. I patrolled the house, then stalked the outside. I wanted to prowl along the fence, but my instincts screamed at me not to leave Jade unprotected.

The first streaks of dawn muddled the sky when one of Superhuman Security's standard black SUVs coasted to a stop in front of the common hall.

I started to go discover what brought our allies to our door, but before I lost sight of my house I'd turned back. I needed to go, but I couldn't leave Jade.

I scooped her sleeping form into my arms, maneuvered her into loose pajamas, and resettled her against my chest before draping a blanket over her.

I met Drym on the path to the hall. He had Kendal wrapped much as Jade was, only she blinked sleepily in his arms.

I'd be alarmed at Jade sleeping through me dressing her and walking in the chilly night air, but she'd admitted that I'd worn her out. Our bond, blinking strong around us, reassured me she was okay.

Cavi joined our group, and by the time we crossed the threshold, all five of my brothers lined up behind me. Inside, we found Bull tapping away at his ever-present computer and Zeus poking a fledgling fire in the fireplace. Neither of them looked particularly alarmed, so my brothers and I relaxed a fraction.

Kragen took point, as usual, and we were happy to let him.

"What brings you to us today, Zeus?"

Bull's head whipped up and he looked around like he'd forgotten where he was.

"We have news on BioSynth." Zeus's eyes flicked to the far side of the room, where Roul stood behind the chair he'd helped Nanna into.

Kragen nodded and then took his own seat at the end of our long, live-edge table. One of the few things we'd kept from the days we lived in a cave just after our escape. The rest of us followed suit, taking our usual spots: Kragen and Drym at the ends, Roul next to Kragen, and me next to Drym. Cavi and Quin sat in the center. They were just as deadly as the rest of us, but they were healers, and we naturally protected them.

Jade burrowed deeper into my chest. Zeus had kept his voice low, perhaps because of our sleeping mates, and I was grateful.

"We were able to follow a low-level scientist north, thanks to a tracker placed on one of the cars Wasp didn't incinerate during Drym's extraction."

Drym had allowed himself to be taken in the hopes we would learn where their new base of operations was. Kendal almost killed us when she realized we had planned for that eventuality. Another member of Superhuman Security, Wasp, helped him escape—again—but his method involved a large amount of explosives.

There wasn't much in the way of clues left behind.

"He eventually stopped over five hundred miles west of here. In satellite images, the area is untouched forest. I sent Colt to poke around a bit, and he found nothing. At least, not on the surface."

I tilted my head to give my good eye line of sight to Roul. I wanted to monitor his mood. I suspected there would be mention of Isabelle, the scientist who helped us escape, and his mate. I wasn't sure what his reaction would be. I shifted Jade slightly to free one arm. Just in case the other was needed to restrain him.

I noticed Kragen angle his chair into a position that would allow him to leave it quickly and suspected it was for the same reason.

"Colt is adept at sensing heat, and there was a lot of it coming from underground. He found a ventilation tunnel and was able to get a sense of the place. It's not as large as the campus you escaped from. About a third of the size. It's not a new base of operations. More like a gathering point to regroup. He said it was lightly staffed, with what appeared to be mostly junior employees."

"You're certain?" Roul's voice was more growl than anything but remained calm.

"Yes." Zeus stared pointedly at Roul. "We've received communication from someone on the inside."

"Isabelle."

Zeus nodded. "She is unharmed. She will try to stay in more regular communication, but it's difficult. General Pierce has increased security to where every employee with even a hint of knowledge about the wyrfang project is monitored around the clock. They are being kept in a large, windowless building in a remote location and not allowed access to communication from the outside."

"She's imprisoned?"

Nanna reached a hand behind her shoulder and closed her fingers around Roul's wrist. He visibly relaxed. I wasn't sure what sort of magic she had, but I silently thanked her for using it to help him.

Zeus's lips quirked. "In a sense. I get the impression that she feels like they're trapped with her instead of the other way around. She's okay, and promised to let us know if that changes." He reached into Bull's laptop bag and pulled out an envelope. He held it out to Roul. "She sent this for you."

For a moment, the envelope hung between them, and we all held our breath. Roul finally took it with a brief glance.

"She also sent valuable information about their new location. They moved employees in blacked-out vans, so she can't be one hundred percent sure, but she thinks they're somewhere in Colorado."

Kragen voiced the question I suspected many of us had. "How does she know even that much?"

Bull was the one who answered. "The same magic she's using to gain access to unrestricted internet has given her a glimpse of what's outside the concrete building. It's not enough to find them, but she thinks given a few weeks she'll be able to pinpoint where they are."

Roul snorted and abandoned his post behind Nanna, disappearing through the door. Cavi stood to go after him, but Nanna's hand pulled him back down.

"Let him go, dearie. He needs to read his letter and calm down a bit."

"What are our next steps?" Kragen got us back on track.

"Unfortunately, all we can do is wait."

As one, the five of us winced. Roul was already unpredictable and moody. We weren't sure how much longer he could wait.

"Now, about Jade…"

TWENTY-NINE

HEARING MY NAME popped my eyes open. I'd been enjoying my perch, wrapped tightly in Thurl's warm arms, his fur soft against my cheek. The indistinct murmur of voices soothed my sleepy brain.

"Now, about Jade..."

That got my attention. "What about me?"

Thurl's arms tightened around me. There were two new people in the hall. One was a wide, bulky man whose eyes were intense. I would never want to meet him in a dark alley. The other was lanky as he slouched in his chair, fingers tapping on a laptop. He had the appearance of someone at ease, but there were tension lines along his muscles. Black ink peeked from beneath his sleeve and above his collar.

"Jade, this is Zeus, owner of Superhuman Security, and their resident tech expert, Bull."

Bull nodded without taking his eyes off his computer screen, but Zeus's eyes took on a warmth I didn't think possible.

"Miss Massey, Thurl asked us to look into the organization troubling you."

I craned my head up and pulled Thurl's muzzle down so I could look him in the eyes. "You did?"

He nodded. "I will use every resource I have to keep you safe."

Wow. That was refreshing. I wasn't used to men acknowledging they needed help, let alone asking for it. But then, these weren't exactly men, were they? I managed to school my expression into something serious. "What did you find?"

"Silver Fang is an up-and-coming organization in Damruck's underworld. I think they see the loss of The Level's leadership as an opportunity. The man you witnessed committing murder is the leader of Silver Fang—Adrian Vale. Respectable businessman by day, he's known as cunning and charismatic, with a sharp mind and predatory instincts. His nickname is The Wolf because he's a calculating hunter.

"I can't figure out why he would be on the street, dressed as a thug, doing wet work himself. He has plenty of assassins in his employ."

"Yeah, I think I met one."

That brought Bull's eyes to mine. "You did, but he's—"

"No longer a threat." Thurl's chest rumbled with his words.

They didn't blink at the pronouncement of the man's death, so either they already knew or didn't care. I wasn't sad he was gone, but I winced. "Did he have family?"

Thurl's cheek rubbed along the side of my head. "No kitten, he did not."

I didn't question him further. He'd never lied to me, and above that, I wanted to believe him. I turned to Bull. "So what do I do now? Wait until they arrest him and testify?"

Bull was shaking his head before I'd finished.

"They won't arrest him. He's too insulated." He sat back in his chair, his fingers still for the first time. "Come to think of it, that could be why he was cosplaying a thug. He's known for having a posh, elegant image. It will be hard to convince someone he would slum it."

Zeus stepped forward. "The best course of action is to remain here, under the wyrfangs' protection."

"I can't stay here forever. I have a job, a house…" My eyes blurred until all I could see were the dancing red motes of light.

Thurl's arms tightened around me again. "Please. Let me protect you." He looked around the table at the others. "Let us protect you."

"Of course I will. I'm not dumb. I'm not about to run off somewhere by myself. But it's not like you can be with me twenty-four/seven. I have a life."

"You do," Zeus nodded, "but our recommendation is that you remain with them—yes, twenty-four/seven—until this is over."

I pushed my glasses back up my nose. "When will this be over? You say they won't arrest this man. You say he'll be able to wiggle himself out of my testimony. So when will it end?"

Everyone fell silent. I let it linger for a beat. "Right. So there has to be a compromise."

Thurl's voice was more growl than anything. "I will not compromise with your safety."

I curled my hand around his neck. "I don't want you to." I sighed and looked around the room. "There has to be another way."

"There is."

When I looked at him, Zeus had transformed into something dark. Menace rolled off him in waves. I clutched at Thurl's forearm. He might be there to help me, but he was frightening.

"You're going to kill him?"

He chuckled, but it wasn't a sound of mirth. "No. I wish we could, but the council wouldn't go for it. Not when there have been so many other, higher-profile problems lately. But…" he paused to look at Thurl. "If Thurl will allow it, I can assign a Superhuman Security operative to your detail."

I heard the rumble deep in the chest I leaned against, but before he could speak, I sat up. "I am a grown woman who can make her own decisions. I don't need his—or anyone's—permission."

Everyone in the room was shaking their heads. It was Kragen who leaned forward and explained.

"It's not about permission, Jade. You are Thurl's mate. That bond is instinctual and overrides everything else. To see another protecting you," he sighed, "it could be problematic."

I stood up so I could look at Thurl properly. I studied his blazing red eyes. "He can handle it." It wasn't a proclamation, but it wasn't a question either.

He stared back at me. "Yes."

Zeus cleared his throat. "I don't mean to pry, but have the two of you bonded?"

I was reluctant to answer him. I'd like to have kept our bond between us, at least for a little while longer. I could feel Thurl looking at me, waiting for me to decide. I pursed my lips. "Yes. We have the tether. I assume that's why you're asking?"

He nodded. "The wyrfang bond, as I understand it, allows either of you to track the other. It means we won't have to worry with a physical tracker for you. As a precaution, of course."

I snorted. "Of course."

Relief that there was a solution to my predicament that didn't involve me hiding in my own shadow flowed through me. His big hand found the small of my back, warm and reassuring. It was crazy how quickly I'd grown used to his casual touches.

"Then it's settled," Zeus said, in a voice that was half-order, half-suggestion. "I'll assign someone, discreetly, who can watch your back when Thurl can't."

Thurl's arm tensed against me, but he didn't argue. I glanced up at him. There was a flicker of conflict in his eyes, like two voices in his head were battling it out. Still, he nodded.

Kragen leaned forward, resting his forearms on the table. "Is there any chance you could find something—evidence, old ledger entries, or a whistleblower testimony—to link him solidly to Vale's illegal dealings? We could approach the council with something compelling enough to force their hand."

I perked up at the good idea.

Bull shook his head, the muscle in his jaw working in annoyance. "He's too careful. I've been searching since Thurl first asked us to poke around. His digital trail is squeaky clean. Anything that might incriminate him is deeply off-book or locked in an analog file, if it exists at all."

I sank into the seat next to Thurl, adjusting my glasses. "So testifying is pointless. The cops can't nail him, and without solid evidence of his wrongdoing, Society can't help either. Great." I tried not to sound completely defeated, but the frustration leaked in anyway.

Bull gave me a lopsided grin. "I'm good at what I do. Given time, I'll find something."

Zeus exhaled, the sound slow and rumbling. He was still standing, arms crossed. "In the meantime, you'll have a bodyguard who will protect you when Thurl can't. We'll secure your house. Make it look lived in, lights on timers, a caretaker going in and out. If Vale's men are watching, they'll see normal movement, but not you."

"I don't like that idea. My friend Elle was attacked feeding the cats because they thought she was me. I don't want anyone else to get hurt."

Zeus smiled. "I'll ask River to housesit for you. If anyone else tries to pull a stunt like that, she'll get a kick out of it."

I didn't quite understand, but from the way Bull chuckled, I guessed this River could handle herself. "What about my job? I can't abandon my kids."

"Returning to work makes you vulnerable and I can't advise it. I have a feeling the detectives will call you in soon. Let's see how that goes, and we can reassess."

"Until then, I'm hiding?"

Zeus's voice gentled. "In my line of work, when the threat is big enough, the best thing to do is disappear for a while."

"For now, it's the wisest move," Kragen added sympathetically.

I swallowed. It wasn't like I wanted to boldly walk down the street, daring these criminals to come at me. But being locked away made me feel like the walls were closing in. Thurl's hand slid up my spine. The warm pressure of his palm was comforting in a way I couldn't quite put into words.

"As soon as we have new intel," Zeus continued, "we'll regroup. Until then, Jade, I'm afraid you need to be patient."

I pursed my lips, but I had to admit it was probably the safest course. "Alright. Do I get to know who this bodyguard is, or is that a surprise?"

A strange smile tugged at Zeus's mouth. "I have someone in mind: a new recruit who's been making waves in the company. She's ex-military, specialized in close-quarters protection, and she won't take up a lot of space in your personal life—unless you need her to. Best of all, she's not about to poke Thurl's territorial instincts."

My eyes flicked to Thurl. His gaze was fixed on Zeus, no small measure of concern in his expression. "How soon can she start?"

"Immediately," Zeus answered. "I'll give you her contact information. If at any time you need or want to leave the compound, call her and she'll be here."

Bull glanced between Thurl and me, then turned the laptop so that I could see a map of Damruck. "We have your work address, your usual routes, and your gym. Did I miss anything?"

I coughed. "You know about my gym membership?"

Bull's brows rose. "We like to be thorough."

"I'll say. I haven't used it once." I appreciated the thoroughness, given the circumstances. "I guess you should add Big Muddy's. I go there way too often."

Bull smiled. "Best burger in town." He typed something quickly. I watched new pins populate the digital map, each one representing a location I frequented. The cluster was bigger than I'd expected—my routine felt so small, yet seeing it all on the screen made me realize just how often I moved around the city. Work, errands, meetups with friends, daily life.

Thurl's hand wrapped around mine. "You won't lose any of it. This is just… a time-out."

I squeezed his fingers. "I know." I looked up at him, letting some of my frustration, my fear, flicker through. "It's just hard."

"You're not alone," he murmured, voice so low it was almost a rumble. "Even if I can't be by your side every second, the bond will let me know if you're in danger."

"And we'll be there," Kragen added. "All of us."

I managed a smile. Maybe I wasn't so helpless after all. Surrounded by Superhuman Security, hulking wyrfangs, and a mate bond that literally let him track me, I might be the safest I'd ever been—even if it felt stifling.

Zeus pocketed his phone. "Luna's up-to-date and she looks forward to meeting you."

"Do you need me for anything else? I think I'd like to go home now." Despite having slept more than usual, exhaustion settled in my bones.

"Try to rest," Zeus said, his eyes sympathetic.

Without asking, Thurl scooped me into his arms again and strode from the common hall.

I looked up at him, marveling at the strength surrounding me with such gentleness. "Thank you. For protecting me."

"You are my mate."

It was a matter-of-fact statement and he seemed to think that explained everything. “Right,” I said softly. “And who protects you, Thurl?”

He skidded to a halt, his muscles bunching where they held me. “No one has ever…” His chest rose and fell with a deep breath. Then his head shook as if to clear it. In a low voice, he answered, “You do, kitten.”

I understood. I couldn’t protect him physically, but he didn’t need me to protect his body. He could do that on his own. What he needed was someone to protect his heart. His soul. He had been through so much, experienced so much trauma, and despite the claws and horns and deadly power, he was vulnerable.

I knew without a doubt he would protect me. And I was determined to protect him right back.

Because from here on out, there was no me or him. There was only us.

THE NEXT MORNING I woke warm and happy in Thurl’s arms, the smell of bacon and eggs permeating the room. “Mmm. Nanna’s made breakfast.”

He shifted and I felt his cold nose against my neck, then his warm tongue as it flicked and trailed over my collarbone.

"Are you hungry?"

I stretched and realized I was naked beneath the covers. I didn't remember getting naked. Thurl's tongue wrapped around my nipple and I moaned.

"I'm getting there."

He chuckled and scraped his teeth along my stomach. My clit pulsed and I rubbed my thighs together. Even though talking with Zeus and Bull yesterday exhausted me, Thurl showed me the fastest way to get my brain to shut up was for him to lick me. That forked tongue could do wicked things and I was addicted.

My skin lit up as he made his way down to where I wanted him most.

"Breakfast is ready, you two!"

For an eighty-year-old woman, Nanna's voice was loud.

"Just a minute!" I yelled back at her, my breath sucking in when Thurl's tongue found my clit.

"It's going to get cold!"

I groaned. Thurl chuckled, nipping my inner thigh.

"We'd better go before she comes to get us."

I wouldn't put it past her, and Thurl had already gotten up, abandoning me still spread eagle on the bed. I groaned in frustration. "Fine."

Just as I stepped into the kitchen my phone rang. Detective Chambers' serious voice greeted me.

"Jade, I'm glad I caught you."

Had he been trying to reach me? I pulled the phone away from my ear to check the notifications, but I didn't see any missed calls or voice mails.

"We need you to come to the station this afternoon," he continued as I put the phone back to my ear. "The district attorney wants to meet with you about your statement."

"Um, okay. What time?"

"Does two work?"

"Yes, I think that's fine."

"I can send a car for you—"

"No, that's not necessary. I'll have a friend drive me. I'll see you then."

"Take care, Jade."

"I will."

I hung up and faced Thurl and my grandmother, who both stared at me with worried expressions. "Detective Chambers says the D.A. wants to talk to me. I'm going in at two."

I kissed the side of Thurl's muzzle when he started growling. "I'm going to text Luna and tell her to pick me up."

He dipped his chin, but I could tell he wasn't happy. Nanna took his hand and led him into the kitchen, telling him she needed help to bring out the dishes. In minutes, the house was once again full of wyrfangs, and I was grateful for the distraction.

LUNA WAS A short, curvy woman with a bright smile and shoulder-length black hair. Her brown skin was flawless and her deep brown eyes sparkled with mischief. She stepped away from the black SUV she'd driven to the compound, her hand outstretched.

"Hi, you must be Jade. It's nice to meet you. I'm Luna, but the boys call me Trouble."

I laughed and shook her hand. "I'm sure they do. You're gorgeous."

Her eyes widened and skittered away. "Oh, thank you, but that's not the kind of trouble I've ever been known for."

She was blushing, and so was I. "I didn't mean to imply that you're … I just meant that …" I stumbled to a stop, not sure how I could dig my way out of that hole. I shook my head and decided not to try. "Sometimes my mouth says things before my brain tells it not to."

She snorted and it put me right at ease. "Now that, I understand." She tilted her head to the car. "Get in. We can talk on the way."

She didn't seem fazed by Thurl standing behind me. I gave him a hug and whispered reassurance that I'd be fine before getting into the passenger seat. I watched him in the side mirror as we drove away. Before we disappeared, he gave a small wave.

I didn't realize how much of a security blanket he'd become until I could no longer see him and my anxiety skyrocketed. I picked at a loose thread on my jeans and tried to tell my brain to settle down. Luna's voice made me jump.

"They are really impressive, aren't they?"

It took a minute for me to catch up. "The wyrfangs? Yes, they are."

"Is this the first time you've been apart since you bonded?"

Cripes, crackers and crickets, did everyone know? "Yes, it is. Will I always feel like this?"

She looked at me in surprise. "I have no idea. Fated mates have only just started happening again."

"Oh, that's right. I forgot."

She nodded and we fell silent for a while.

"Can I ask you a question?" Her voice was timid, which didn't match her appearance at all.

"Of course."

"What's it like? Having a fated mate?"

I laughed. How could I possibly answer that? "Well, I've only been one for about a week, so I'm no expert. But it's like having part of yourself walking around outside of your body. I know people say that about kids, but this is different somehow. When I'm with him, there's a sense of peace, of rightness, that I've never felt before. I was terrified of being tied to him forever, but now that I am it seems silly for me to think there was ever another choice."

She nodded and parked in front of the police station. "Thank you. So many of us never dared to dream about finding a mate. It's been so long… but now there's hope." She grinned. "And a lot of questions and nerves to go along with it."

I smiled back. "I can imagine."

Her face went serious, like a switch had been flipped. "While we're in there, don't go anywhere without me. We're just friends, and I'm there to support you, but I'm your security blanket in Thurl's absence. Don't let them separate us."

I nodded. "Got it."

I couldn't imagine Detective Chambers or his partner trying to separate us. They'd both been nice to me. Her presence seemed to keep the panic beneath the surface, but as we walked through the front door I felt my muscles tighten.

Luna grabbed my hand. “You got this.”

“Okay.” I focused on breathing as we made our way to the detective’s floor. Chambers was leaning against a nearby metal desk when we stepped off the elevator.

“I’m glad you brought someone with you this time. How are you?”

“About like you’d expect.”

He mock grimaced. “That good, hunh?”

“How is Elle?” I talked to her on the phone, but hadn’t been able to see her since her attack, and I felt awful. She assured me she was fine, but it was still my fault she got hurt.

I tilted my head when a blush spread across his cheeks. “She’s good. I’ve checked in on her a couple times. She’s a strong lady.”

When I wasn’t knee deep in shit, I’d have to ask her why the detective blushed.

He led us into the same spare conference room I’d been before, but this time, there was another man besides Detective Drake. Balding and somewhat round, his face held a world-weary expression but he smiled as we walked in.

“Ms. Massey, it’s nice to finally meet you. I’m Bradley Laurent, the district attorney here in Tayki county.”

His hand was slightly clammy and I resisted the urge to wipe my palms on my jeans. "Not an assistant, then?"

He shook his head. "This case deserves my attention. Please, have a seat."

We sat, and for the next hour and a half, I answered questions. Laurent was no nonsense and seemed competent enough. The hope that Vale would be arrested—so thoroughly smashed the day before—started coming back to life. Surely this man wouldn't just let him walk.

As the interview drew to a close, he sat forward.

"One more thing, Ms. Massey. How is your eyesight without your glasses?"

"Dismal, but I was wearing them that night."

"And you're sure you can positively identify the man you saw?"

"Yes. Like I told Detective Chambers, I don't believe anything is one hundred percent, but that is the man I saw that night."

"There wasn't enough light for him to see you."

"No, but I was next to a dumpster at the end of the alley, and he was at the entrance where the streetlights were."

"I see."

He stood and I followed suit. We shook hands. He thanked me for my time, and then he left. To be honest, it was a little anti-climactic. I thought maybe he would tell me they were going to arrest Vale right away on the strength of my witness statement. Maybe that only happened on TV.

I excused myself to go to the bathroom before we left. Luna followed, but stayed outside the door of the small, one-toilet restroom. The actual toilet was enclosed in a partition, with the sink beside it, which seemed weird, but I guess it was so if someone was peeing another person could wash their hands.

As soon as I pushed open the door of the partition a dark shape flew at me, slammed me into the wall and pressed their forearm into my neck. I struggled against their hold, but they were strong and I started seeing stars. I tried to yell, but couldn't. In a desperate attempt to make any noise at all, I swung my leg to the side and hit the enclosure door, causing it to thwack against the wall.

I slid to the floor when the pressure left my neck. Luna fought with my attacker in my peripheral vision, but it wasn't long before she knelt in front of me. She turned my head from side to side as I winced.

"I don't think there's any serious damage. You'll have one hell of a bruise, but you're breathing. How's your eyesight?"

"Blurry." At some point, my glasses had been knocked off my face. Luna retrieved them and slid them on.

"How about now?"

I nodded. "Good. Fine. No more black spots."

I didn't notice the other people crowded into the bathroom until I looked up. Detective Chambers held the elbow of my attacker—a woman now that her hood was down and I could see her face. He shouted questions at her without waiting for an answer.

"Who are you? How did you get in here? Who sent you?"

The woman laughed, a manic sound that chilled my blood. Her eyes were wide, and her arms strained against the restraints. Before I registered what was happening. she'd broken free of his hold and slammed her head into the side of the sink. She managed another two hits before Chambers and Drake pulled her out of the room.

I stared at Luna in shock.

She shook her head. "Drugs."

I nodded, struck mute by all that happened.

She stood and tugged me up with her. "Let's get you out of here."

"I still need to pee."

She laughed and tugged me behind her. "We'll find you another bathroom. And this time, I'm coming in with you."

THIRTY

"THURL, I NEED to breathe."

Jade's muffled voice came from my chest, where I had her smooshed against me. I couldn't let her go, couldn't make my muscles unlock where I held her.

She turned her head to the side and took a deep breath.

"I'm okay."

Her small hand patted and stroked my lower back.

"I'm okay," she repeated.

"I *felt* it, Jade." Emotion strangled my throat.

"I know. It's okay now."

At that moment, I wanted to say it would never be okay again. I knew I was overreacting. I had already been on edge with her gone, but when the pressure slammed into my neck I went into the fog. Every thought emptied from my head save one—get to Jade.

The stranglehold lasted mere seconds, but I'd made it to the fence when it loosened. My brothers surrounded me, having heard my roar when I took off. My brain kicked in when Roul grabbed my arm. I snapped at him, but stilled when he spoke.

"Tell us where we're going."

They weren't questioning me or my need to get to her. I shook my head to clear it further and a phone rang. As one, our heads swiveled to look at Quin.

"What? We have allies now. It would be stupid not to carry a phone." He pulled it from a small pack that was fastened around his waist. "Hello?" He listened and then looked at me. "It's Luna. Jade's fine. There was an incident at the police station, but it's been handled. They're on their way back now."

When the SUV pulled through the gates, I nearly ripped the door from the hinges to get her into my arms. I heard the others talking, but my heart still pounded in my ears. "I can't lose you."

"You won't, Thurl. I'm right here. Luna was with me. She saved me. I was protected."

I snapped when a hand fell on my back. Drym backed away, his hands up in surrender.

"Take her home. You need to see that she is safe and unharmed."

I shivered as the thoughts of what might have happened continued to torment my brain. She didn't protest when I picked her up, but I felt her waving at the others behind my back as we left. I didn't need to stay to discuss the incident. I knew Drym was right, and they would fill me in later.

Nanna stopped us just inside the door. "Oh my god, baby, what happened?"

"I'm okay Nanna. I was attacked in the bathroom at the police station, but I'm okay now."

She smoothed Jade's hair from her face. "Was it Silver Fang?"

"We don't know yet. Luna and Detective Chambers are looking into it."

"Do you want me to go to Roul's?"

It took a minute before I understood she was asking me. "Only if you wish."

"I'll go then. Let me know if you need me, honey." She patted me and Jade at the same time.

"Thanks, Nanna."

I sat on the edge of the bed with Jade still wrapped in my arms.

"What can I do to help?"

I snorted. "Never leave my sight again."

She sighed and pulled away from me but stayed on my lap. "That's no life for either of us."

My heart clenched, and I resisted the need to pull her back against me. She slid from my lap, standing between my legs when my hands compulsively gripped her thighs.

"I'm not leaving you."

"I know, but—."

"No buts, Thurl. I'm not leaving you."

"You already chafe against my hold. I am a monster, and you will grow tired of me, of my need to protect you." I looked into her eyes. "My need for you."

She cupped my face in her hands. "I chose you, Thurl. I choose you."

I looked away. "You say that now, when you are frightened. What happens when the threat is gone? What happens when all that's left is a monster who can't live by your side in daylight?"

"I will still choose you."

"You can't know that."

She grunted in frustration. "How can such a powerful creature be so dense?"

I felt like I'd been slapped.

"Oh, don't look at me like that. Close your mouth before you catch flies. You are amazing, Thurl. You are a beast, that's true, but you're also kind and gentle. You're considerate and passionate. Generous and loyal."

"I was bred to kill."

She nodded. "And I'm sure you're good at it. That doesn't mean you aren't capable of love, or worthy of it."

I swallowed. "What I feel for you…" my heart squeezed. I felt like I stood at the edge of a cliff. Her reaction to what I said next meant everything. Our bond lights flared around us. "I love you, Jade."

"I love you, too, Thurl. And love means it will all work out. Our love—our bond—will make it work."

Her words sank beneath my skin, burrowed into my heart, and took up residence in my soul. Not that I wanted to believe her, or needed to, but that I had to. She forced them on me with certainty enough for both of us. The lingering doubts about not being good enough for her, not being what she needed, dissolved in the face of her love.

"You are truly okay? Your neck isn't sore? You don't need to be seen by a doctor?"

"An EMT checked me over at the station. My neck is tender, and will be for a few days, but I'll be fine."

I gave her a tiny nod. "I need you. I need to feel you wrapped around me, my cock inside you thrumming with your heartbeat and squeezed by your orgasms."

She sucked in a breath. "Yes, please."

She pulled her shirt over her head and toed off her shoes while I pulled her jeans down her body. The scent of her arousal wrapped me in a delicious hold and I groaned as my dick pushed from my seam. Her small hand grabbed me and it jerked in her hold. I tugged her wrist away. "I will not last."

"That's okay."

"I won't be able to control myself. I will hurt you."

"No, you won't. Please, Thurl, I need to feel alive. I need you to fuck me."

I twitched, the need to protect her warring with the need to claim her, to imprint my body, my scent, on her. She grabbed my cock again and yanked hard.

I lost control. I growled low as I spun us around and pinned her to the bed. She cried out when I pushed into her, but I was too far gone to stop. I was more animal than rational, and I rutted her like one. I pounded into her, my hand above her shoulder, holding her in place. Her moans and cries spurred me on.

I sank deep and her walls fluttered around me.

"Oh fuck, I'm close."

I hammered into her, my release threatening, but I held it at bay. I snaked my tail between us and pressed against her clit. With a moaning cry I felt her pussy clamp and squeeze my cock and I exploded. I spilled into her until I felt it leaking out as I slowed my thrusts, easing us both down.

I collapsed to the side, rolling her until she lay limp across my chest. Our juices ran from our still-connected bodies, and I smiled. She chose me. This exquisite creature that I did not deserve chose me.

"Holy shit, Thurl."

"Are you okay?"

She chuckled. "I won't walk for a day or two, but it was worth it."

She wiggled, and my cock responded. She sat up on my chest and stared at me with wide eyes.

"Are you serious? How do you have anything left in the tank after that?"

I squinted in confusion. "What tank?"

She collapsed back onto me. "What tank, he asks. Pete's sake. The sex tank. The well of whatever that makes your dick hard."

"You make my dick hard."

She laughed. "Clearly."

"Do you have nothing left in this tank?"

"Nope." She snorted. "My tank is bone dry."

I tilted my head. "How do I fill it?"

She laughed so hard she fell off my chest. Between snorts she managed to say, "I think you filled it all right."

I was even more confused, but she couldn't answer any further questions. She was laughing too hard.

THIRTY-ONE

KENDAL WAS LAUGHING so hard she nearly fell out of her chair. My sides were hurting, and every now and again, I had to bend backward to release the cramp in my stomach.

"He did not!"

"Oh, he really did."

"What did you say?"

"I said I thought he'd filled that tank already." Tears ran down my face and only squeaks escaped my lips I was laughing so hard.

We sobered when Drym and Thurl walked into the common hall where Kendal invited me to chat. She said she was going stir crazy. I felt horrible when she explained that the whole compound was on lockdown since my attack. No one in or out except for Luna and Zeus.

She waved away my concern. "Don't worry about it. It's no great hardship to stay locked up with Drym." She gave me a look, clearly holding in laughter. "When my well isn't dry."

Drym looked at Thurl. "What does that mean?"

Thurl shrugged. "I still don't know."

In a conspiratorial stage whisper, I said to Kendal, "Don't tell them."

"Never," she said back.

Drym furrowed his brow. "I'm not sure I appreciate all the giggling if I'm the butt of the joke," he said, leaning closer to Kendal.

Kendal shot me a mischievous grin, but played innocent. "It's more of an inside joke," she said, patting Drym's hand. Then, turning to Thurl in mock seriousness, she added, "Don't worry, it's nothing that impacts our security."

Thurl arched a brow, arms folding across his broad chest. "If it did, I'm sure we'd know," he said, his tone so serious that Kendal and I burst out laughing all over again. Thurl glanced at

Drym, shrugged, and then shook his head. "Human jokes," he murmured, as if that explained everything.

"Actually," Kendal said, trying—and failing—to maintain a straight face, "we were discussing the importance of… uh… hydration." She caught my eye, and we both struggled not to dissolve into hysterics once more.

Drym's ears perked. "You've got to stay hydrated," he agreed earnestly, as if offering profound wisdom. "It's key to peak performance."

His unwitting addition to our joke sent us into another round of guffaws and snorts.

After a bit, I managed to squeak out, "Words to live by." I turned to Kendal. "What should we do this afternoon?"

She tapped her lip. "I'd say invite the girls over and booze it up, but I don't think Kragen will go for that."

I tilted my head at her. "The girls?"

"Oh!" She sat up, excited. "Virginia and Gaelynn. They're mated to some of the Supe Sec guys. There are still so few of us, they started a club. The Society Mates Club. Don't worry, you'll love them. I'm sure Virginia will get you a shirt."

"There are shirts?"

She grinned as she nodded. "Jerseys, actually. Remind me and I'll show you mine."

I nodded, dumbstruck by the idea that there were so few mates they'd started a club. I guess I should have known after reading the binder, but it didn't fully register.

Kendal mused about our afternoon plans. "How about a movie marathon? Drym and I have all the streaming channels and a huge sectional that will fit both the guys. We'll pop popcorn and just veg out."

"That sounds amazing."

"Okay, then it's settled."

She stood up and I followed her while our mates trailed behind. Kendal kept up an easy stream of conversation. I looked over my shoulder to find Thurl keeping a close eye on me and smiled as the bond lights wove and bounced between us.

"Do you have the lights, too?" I asked as we walked.

"Yes, they're so pretty. Like stars or fireflies."

"I think they look like embers that escaped from a wood fire."

She stopped as she opened her front door. "Wait, what color are they?"

"Red. What color are yours?"

"Gold." She looked over at our mates to include them in the conversation. "The bond lights match your eyes."

Drym and Thurl looked at each other in surprise. Drym tilted his head. "Yours aren't gold?"

Thurl copied the movement. "Yours aren't red?"

Drym shook his head. "We'll need to tell Bacon. She'll want to add that to the information she's compiling on us."

I perked up at the name. "I like Bacon. She seems nice."

Kendal nodded. "She is, but her familiar can be a lot."

"Her familiar?" I needed to brush up on Society terminology. Thurl mentioned there were more binders. Maybe I could borrow them.

"Yeah, Meanosaurus is a talking chicken with a big attitude."

I blinked. "A… talking… chicken?"

Kendal laughed. "Yep. That was my reaction, too."

We'd made it to the couch, so I tucked my legs under me and settled against the plush cushions. Thurl draped me with a throw blanket.

"I'll make the popcorn," Kendal said over her shoulder as she made her way into the kitchen. She was pulling out an air popper when she exclaimed, "Oh! And have you seen a dragon? There are honest to God dragons."

"No, but Thurl said they have dragon DNA so I figured they exist. Does that mean all the things we thought were myths actually exist?" My mind spun.

"Well," she called, her voice muffled from inside a cabinet, "I can't say if there are unicorns, but the major ones like vampires, and shifters of course, are definitely real."

"Elves?" I squeaked.

"Fae, definitely, but I haven't seen any that look like Legolas, sadly." She winked at me and poured kernels into the popper.

I thought my world exploded when I witnessed a murder in a dark alley. It had, but that was a firework compared to the nuclear blast of finding myself submerged into a whole new universe. It was like the world had tilted on its axis and everything I thought I knew about it was wrong. "I don't think I'll ever get used to this."

The next two minutes were filled with the sounds of popping corn, but when they petered out Kendal flopped onto the couch and offered me a big bowl. "You will. It just takes some getting used to. But look at it this way, even Society didn't know about wyrfangs until a little bit ago, so you can assume you've already met the most fantastical among them."

Somehow, I doubted that. Surely there was a supernatural that out weirded the 'fangs, but I stayed silent and leaned against my own fantastical beast who warmed my side and stole my popcorn.

***

I fell asleep about when Jupiter was embarrassed after telling Caine she'd always liked dogs. I woke up in our bed at Thurl's house.

I'd always been a heavy sleeper, but being here made it ridiculous. I'd never had this sense of peace and safety before. My brain and body were completely on board with letting the wyrfang take the wheel. Even if it meant going to sleep in one place and waking up in an entirely different one.

I smiled at the flickers of red that danced out the door. I dressed and followed them, slowing when I heard Thurl's low voice coming from the living room.

"It's all right. I'm not going to hurt you."

I peeked around the corner and my heart swelled until it burst. Thurl crouched on the floor, Pawssanova curled in his lap, Sir Purrs-a-lot perched on his shoulder like a fluffy orange gargoyle, and Whisker was draped over his tail, legs splayed and belly on full display like the slut he was.

Three feet from Thurl's outstretched hand sat Catzilla. The only person the Bengal tolerated was me, but he sat there slow blinking at Thurl. He didn't make a sound. Not the hiss that was his go-to whenever anything got too close. Not the yowling growl he trotted out when he really meant business, and not the spit and swipe that happened when both were ignored.

I caught Thurl's ear twitch in my direction and smiled when he turned his muzzle to look at me directly. "I think you're winning him over."

He turned back to the cat and tilted his head. "Do you think so?"

"I do." I sauntered into the room and ran my hand down Sir's back before tracing across to Thurl's unoccupied shoulder.

My phone rang on the kitchen counter, startling us both, and triggering the hiss from Catzilla I'd expected. I rolled my eyes at the cat. "Oh come on, Zilla. It's not like you've never heard my phone ring."

A woman's voice I didn't recognize greeted me across the line.

"Jade?"

"Yes, who is this?"

"Hi, I'm River. I work with Zeus at Superhuman Security."

"Oh, right. You're housesitting for me. I hope I didn't leave dirty underwear lying around."

She laughed. "No dirty underwear, and far less cat hair than I expected."

"That's surprising, for sure. What can I do for you?"

Thurl's warm hand skirted across my lower back and curled around my side. I leaned back into him, letting my shoulders drop from my ears. My neck protested. I was going to need a massage after this was over.

"I just wanted to let you know you had another unwanted visitor early this morning."

I gasped, but she kept going before I could interrupt her with the million and one questions that wanted to spill out of me like a two-liter Coke stuffed with Mentos.

"It's fine, the threat was neutralized," her chuckle sent a shiver over me, "and I didn't damage anything. I already informed Zeus, who contacted Kragen, so the whole team knows. You're safe where you are."

"So stay with the wyr—"

She cut me off with a volume that made me take the phone from my ear.

"Yes, you're safe, but your phone isn't secure, and we have to assume the bad guys are competent enough to be listening."

My cheeks heated. "Oh, right. Sorry."

"Don't apologize. This isn't a normal situation, and you have no reason to be thinking about things like that. That's what we're for. Just keep your head down and you'll be fine."

I heard a pained groan in the background. "What was that?"

Once again, her low laugh sounded evil. "Your unwanted guest." She seemed to be speaking to herself when she added, "I didn't expect him to wake up so soon."

Another voice called out. "Damn it, River! We're going to have to sand her floors to get that out!"

"They're real hardwoods. It'll be fine."

I had no idea what was happening at my house, but I was positive I didn't want to know.

"Don't worry, Jade. You'll never know I was here."

"Um… okay."

"Stay safe, and when you see Zeus next, flick his ear for me."

I would absolutely not be doing that. The line went dead with a click, and I set my phone back on the counter.

"Are you okay?"

Thurl's fingers curled tighter around my side, pulling me until our bodies melded from shoulder to thigh. Mine, not his. The top of my head barely reached his chest.

"Yeah, I guess. There was an incident at my house."

"I heard."

I spun out of his hold and stared at him. "What do you mean, you heard? River didn't seem that loud."

"She wasn't. I have excellent hearing."

I put my hands on my hips. "Just how excellent? Have you been eavesdropping on everything I've said since I got here?" My conversations with Kendal ghosted through my mind and my stomach flipped. No wonder he'd been so unsure around me. He'd heard me being unsure about him.

His nose swung back and forth, his ears plastered to his head. "No! I would have to be focused on you. I don't multitask well."

I huffed. "Fine." I let my hands drop. "So how good is your hearing? Can you hear a bug move from a mile away or something?"

"Not quite that good," he chuckled. "But…" He tilted his head and we both went quiet. "I can hear the insect that is bumping into the porch column."

"Holy shit. What about your other senses? Taste, smell, sight?"

He leaned into my neck and inhaled, making me giggle as both his cold nose and his breath tickled.

"I can smell your sugar scent, the spice that lingers from your arousal, the undercurrent of me on your skin."

"Okay, that's hot." I let my head fall to the side to give him better access.

His tongue licked from my collarbone to the curve of my ear. "You taste delicious, like Nanna's snickerdoodles, but better. You are my favorite thing to eat."

And I was soaked. How he could take me from needing coffee to wide awake and wanting in five seconds was a talent I'd never tire of. "And sight?" The words left me on a sigh.

He grunted. "My sight is … impaired."

That threw an ice cube down the back of my shirt. I stepped away and pointed to my glasses. "So is mine."

He looked away from me. "No aid can help in my case."

On my tiptoes, I traced the scar that ran through his eye. "Will you tell me what happened? You don't have to."

He pulled me into his arms, his muzzle rubbing along my back. It was my favorite place to be, surrounded by his strength and warmth. I wrapped my arms as far around his waist as I could and rubbed my nose on his chest.

"They sent us on a mission. We thought the objective was simple: breach a house and take out its occupants. But that was just what they told us. The real aim had been to test us when things went wrong. Until that point, we were flawless. Our missions carried out without incident. It was 'too easy' and they needed to up the difficulty.

"So they sent us with faulty equipment. A flash grenade on the shoulder strap of my tactical vest exploded, sending shrapnel into my face."

I squeezed harder. "That's so cruel."

"Quin patched me up in the field and Cavi did what he could when we returned, but my eyesight was lost."

"Is that why it's dimmer than the other?"

He nodded. "Cavi thought it might cease to glow altogether, but so far its light has just dimmed. Even so, I am damaged."

I stepped back and grabbed his muzzle to force him to look at me. "You are perfect."

He wiggled his head from side to side, and I yanked. "Perfect. Do you hear me? You're amazing."

"I am broken."

I growled and it surprised both of us, but I was so angry. At the scientists whose treatment of them was inhuman, unethical, and evil. And at him, for thinking he was less than. "Do you think me damaged, broken?"

"No!"

"Then neither are you! How can you even think that? You've worshiped my body like I've never experienced. You've opened your home to me and a dozen cats. You make me feel safe." I took a deep breath. "Loved."

His eyes closed as if to hide, since I wouldn't let him pull his face away.

"Nothing about you is damaged or broken."

I released him.

"You are."

I got angry all over again. Was he calling me broken? "I am what?" I snarled at him and his eyes snapped open.

"Loved."

Well, that put a hole in my barrel. I speared my fingers through the fur at his neck. "So are you."

I grabbed his wrist, turned for the stairs, and tugged with all my weight in a futile attempt to get him to move. Coffee be damned.

"What…?"

I didn't bother looking back at him. "I want you to fuck me, Thurl."

I was leaned so far over I would have face planted if he hadn't scooped me up.

He pressed my back against the wall, his breath hot against my ear as his whisper sent a shudder through me.

"Fuck you, kitten?"

"Yes." Raw, unfiltered need laced my words.

His claws pricked as they flexed against my hips. Suddenly, I was free. The cool air that rushed where his warmth had been made me want to scream in frustration, but when I looked at him I could see the fire licked at him, too. His fingers flexed and fisted and for several breaths we stood, staring and panting.

"You should not ask me such things. You should run from me, kitten. I am a monster."

Yep, these panties were goners. "You're *my* monster. And right now, I want the beast."

He growled, the sound filling the room and hitting my chest like a caress.

"Then run."

It took a heartbeat for me to process what he was saying. Then I took off. I raced up the stairs and blindly into our room but I was caught. He tackled me onto the bed, looming over me like the beast he claimed to be.

Caged by his arms, he pushed his knee between my legs, and it made its way slowly up until it was flush against my greedy sex. I ground myself against him, seeking the friction I so badly wanted.

"You are perfect."

His words were laced with wonder, but I didn't want compliments. "What I am is turned on beyond belief and sure that if I don't orgasm in the next few seconds, I'll die."

His claws made quick work of my clothes and with his palm at my sternum, holding me down, his hot mouth attacked my pussy.

Luckily for my life expectancy, I came within seconds. I caught my breath as he hovered over me. With a mischievous grin, I swung my leg and used all my strength to push him over. I straddled his hips and rubbed myself up and down his hard cock like a bitch in heat.

He moaned, and his eyes shuttered. "Jade, please."

A heady sense of power rushed through me. I did this. I made a monster beg.

I slid up, pressed the tip of him at my entrance, but moved with him as he tried to surge up. He growled in frustration.

"You like this."

It wasn't a statement, but I answered him anyway. "Oh yes." I lowered an inch and we both moaned. Slowly I sank, the sensation of fullness overwhelming as I bottomed out. I lifted and sank back down, but it wasn't enough. Out of breath, I said, "Okay, you take over. I need your beast, Thurl."

I was under him so fast it made me dizzy.

"Gladly."

He wasted no time, thrusting into me with a punishing rhythm. My body coiled, spiraling ever higher, spurred on by the sound of him pounding into me and my own moans.

"Thurl," I begged, his name a plea on my lips.

His speed increased and I lost my mind. The tip of his tail pushed at my clit and swirled circles around it with delicious pressure. I fisted his fur and hung on as I shattered like fine crystal. The lights of our bond blazed incandescent around us, lighting the room in fire.

My throat closed and my mouth opened in a silent scream as he kept my orgasm going like the Energizer bunny. Even the feel of his cock pulsing with his own release set me off. Or maybe I hadn't stopped. At that point, I couldn't tell. My brain had been deprived of oxygen for too long and all I knew was searing pleasure.

I floated so high I thought I'd never come down, but my lungs remembered their job and I gulped air like a guppy.

Thurl rolled to my side, the pads of his fingers tracing lazy circles on my stomach. I chilled as sweat cooled from my body. I had never been so bold. I should be embarrassed, but I wasn't. It was Thurl, and…

"I love you."

He jerked like I'd slapped him. I rolled into him and placed a gentle kiss on his pec.

"I choose you."

THIRTY-TWO

ALL MANNER OF qualifiers ran through my head at her words, but then I looked at her. Jade's eyes were fierce.

"I can see what you're thinking. Stop. I choose you, Thurl. I love you."

I couldn't speak, the force of my emotions overwhelming. I pulled her into my arms and cradled her like the precious thing she was.

Muffled in my chest, she said, "I'm covered in drying sweat and cum is leaking out of me. I want a shower."

I let her go and she flopped onto her back.

"Nevermind, I'm too tired to move."

With a chuckle, I scooped her up and carried her into the bathroom. I eyed the tub, considering.

"Shower, please, Thurl. I don't want to sit in this in a tub."

The shower was roomy enough for both of us, but I was apprehensive. The tub had been fine, but no water had been spraying on me.

Her small hand patted my chest.

"It's okay. Put me down. I can shower by myself."

No. I wanted to wash her. I had exhausted her and I had strength enough for both of us. I shook my head and stepped forward, only to be stymied by the unfamiliar controls.

She flicked the water on for me, only to squeal as it came out cold. I jumped back, out of the stream, my heart racing faster than it should. She pet me again.

"It's okay, the water just needs to warm up."

She put her fingers under the spray, and after a moment, she nodded.

"Okay. It's warm now."

I carried her into the enclosure, thankful I had opted for one that was large enough to not need a door over the opening. I set her on her feet under the spray. At first, I held her out, trying to have as little of me in the water as possible, but when she sighed happily and relaxed, so did I.

By the time I had soaped and rinsed us both, I was at ease. I didn't think a shower would ever be a favorite activity of mine, but I no longer feared the experience.

"Shall I put you in bed?"

She laughed. "I think I need coffee. If I go back to sleep, I'll be up late tonight."

Voices filtered up to us and I picked out individuals. "Nanna is here with Roul. There is also a woman I don't recognize."

"Really? I can't hear a thing."

I licked the side of her face and she swiped at her cheek with a giggle.

"Are you sure they didn't put dog DNA in you?"

I nipped her earlobe and growled.

She laughed and pushed at my chest. When I finished drying myself, I found her in our bedroom getting dressed. She pulled a soft shirt that hugged her curves over her head. Her eyes twinkled with laughter. I wondered how I could thank the fates for her.

Downstairs I assessed the strange woman I'd heard. She was compact and well muscled. Straight black hair framed upturned eyes that seemed to see everything.

Nanna came forward and grabbed Jade's hands.

"Jade! I thought y'all would never come down. Meet River. This lovely young lady has been looking after your house while you're away."

"Yes, it's so nice to meet you."

Jade strode to the woman with an outstretched hand, and I resisted the urge to pull her back. There was a feral edge to River. Despite her size, she was dangerous.

"I wanted to drop by and introduce myself so you can put a face to the name and voice staying in your house."

"Thank you, I appreciate that. You're okay? After what happened this morning?"

She scoffed. "Not a scratch, promise."

"I'm so glad."

I relaxed. River was definitely a threat, but not to Jade.

"Nanna was telling me you were with Kendal watching movies last night."

Jade's face lit up with a smile. "That's right."

"Next time, call me. I have a Seductflix account." River waggled her eyebrows. "And I make the best popcorn."

Jade laughed. "I will, promise."

"Have you met the others yet?"

I thought of the Superhuman Security males and growled. River smirked at me.

"Relax, big guy, I'm talking about the other mates."

"I haven't, but Kendal's told me about them. I guess there really are only a few of us, hunh?"

"Just the four of you, so far." She sighed and put a hand on her chest, looking up at the ceiling. "The rest of us are still seeking." She straightened and smiled at Jade. "At least we have hope now, thanks to you and the others."

"How long was it," I asked, "before Virginia?"

"We think for the bulk of shifters it was centuries. There've been rumors that have circulated through the years of one or two shifters finding their mates, but never more than that and always unsubstantiated."

I couldn't imagine the horror of never finding Jade, but so many must have gone through just that. Jade verbalized my thoughts.

"That's awful."

River shrugged. "It was what it was, but now it's not."

Nanna broke the melancholy. "Come on everybody, I've got brunch waiting at Roul's."

River hesitated. "I should get back to Jade's house."

"Nonsense! Her house will keep, and you have to eat."

River shook her head, but Nanna didn't let her say another word.

"Roul, pick her up and cart her ass if she won't come willingly."

River threw her hands up in surrender as Roul stepped toward her. "Okay, okay, fine! No need to sick scary on me, sheesh."

I thought I was the only one who noticed Roul's wince until Jade wrapped an arm around his waist.

"He's not scary. He's a big marshmallow. They all are." She reached up and patted his cheek.

My chest ached with a swell of love. Roul may be the biggest, the deadliest of us, but he was also fragile. And my mate defended him. I didn't deserve her, but I would work every second for the rest of my life in the hope one day I might.

THIRTY-THREE

WE WERE HALFWAY through brunch when Luna arrived. She hugged me and gave River a fist bump.

"I saw the dude from this morning. You're vicious, River."

River laughed. "His mistake, breaking into Jade's house like that." She shrugged.

Now I really didn't want to know what happened in my living room in the wee hours of the morning.

"Ghost is still grumbling about sanding the floor."

"Not like he'll be the one doing it."

They both dissolved in laughter, and a pang hit my chest. I hadn't had many close girlfriends. Kendal had been lovely, but I didn't know if she liked me or if I was just the only other human on the compound. I wasn't good at making friends. I talked too much, had little to no filter, and a dozen cats. None of which lent to easy friendships.

"Did you know about the movie sleepover last night?"

Luna's eyes cut to mine. "There was a movie sleepover last night? And you didn't invite us?"

I blushed and stammered. "Um… no…?"

Luna playfully swatted my arm. "I'm messing with you. But for real, if there's another one, invite us. River has a Seductflix account and whoo!" She fanned her face.

"I already told her," River said from across the table.

Luna nodded. "Good. Plus, she makes the best popcorn. She eats it basically all the time, so she should."

"Told her that, too."

I gave them both a genuine smile. "I will. I'd like that."

River cut her eyes at Luna. "I'm here because I wanted to introduce myself. Why are you here?"

"Oh! Right." Luna turned back to me. "The D.A. wants to talk to you again."

My brows scrunched. "Why didn't he call me?"

"He tried, but I guess you left your phone at Thurl's?"

I patted my back pocket and found it empty. "Damn, I did."

"It's okay. He called me when he couldn't get hold of you since I gave him my number the other day." She tilted her head toward the door. "Are you ready? I parked the SUV at the hall."

None of the 'fangs houses had roads that led to them. The only driveway in or out of the compound stopped at the common hall. There was a small parking area, big enough to hold maybe four of the SUVs Supe Sec favored, plus the 'fang's van that Kendal drove.

"Sure. Let me run by Thurl's for my phone and my purse."

I felt him stiffen under my hand. I stood up and he followed suit. I gave him a hug that ended with a pat on his bicep. "Stay here. Visit with your brothers." Naturally, they had all shown up for Nanna's feast. "Luna will be with me."

He looked around at the others. "If you're sure?"

"I'm sure. I'll be fine. Nanna will pass out the after-meal cookies soon. I'll be back before you know it."

He acquiesced, and I let out a breath. He'd been at my side every second I was here. He needed to spend some time with his brothers without me underfoot.

Luna chatted about nothing while we gathered my things, but when I slid into the passenger seat with her, she turned serious. "I'm not happy about this meeting. He wants me to bring you to what he called a satellite office. He said it's more secure, but it's sketchy. In the warehouse district. If I tell you to run, you run. If I tell you to duck, get your ass down. Got it?"

"I got it." And there were my nerves, poking holes in the calm I'd managed to accumulate. "If you have a bad feeling, why are we going?"

She shrugged. "He insisted, and Bull said he checked out. I trust that Bull would have found something if he was dirty."

"Okay." I wrung my hands in my lap until she reached over and put her palm over them to stop me.

"You'll be fine. I'll make sure of it."

I relaxed and tried to smile. "I know." I trusted her. That was the problem—something felt off about this to her, and so the whole thing seemed like a bad idea to me. Her instincts amplified mine a thousand fold.

The warehouse we parked in front of almost triggered a panic attack.

The outside looked like a can that was tied behind a 'just married' car. After the newlyweds came back from the honeymoon. Which was a road trip through the mountains of Appalachia.

Weeds had taken over what was left of the asphalt in the parking lot and the security fence wouldn't keep out a raccoon. A crumbling dock was being slowly eaten by the Blackgum river. A single security light hung next to the door, doing its best impression of Eeyore.

I was about to put my butt right back in the car when the door opened, revealing Bradley Laurent in all his balding glory. He looked left and then right, like he was a bouncer at a speakeasy.

"Ms. Massey, please, come in."

I looked at Luna, who nodded, so I started forward, uncertainty lacing every step. He closed the door behind us as I gawked. Inside, it was a whole different world. Spotless, with workspaces scattered throughout the massive space. A large, open area dominated the center and whiteboards on wheels sprang from the floor like spines on a cactus.

My attention snagged on one that held a series of pictures, mostly men's mug shots, with lines drawn between them like a conspiracy board straight from a movie.

The top picture was Adrian Vale.

"Welcome to the headquarters of the joint Damruck and F.B.I. task force."

"Wow." It was all I knew how to say at that point.

He chuckled. "We've been working on taking down the crime organizations in Damruck for years. The leaders of which have remained out of our grasp…" He looked over his shoulder at me while he led us further into the building. "Until now."

"It's my understanding that Adrian Vale is powerful and connected enough to discredit me and any testimony I might give."

He shined his bald pate with the sweat of his palm. "That's possible, but your testimony is the closest we've come to having a solid case on any of them. I plan to prosecute him for murder based on your eyewitness account, Ms. Massey."

My eyebrows joined my hairline. "So you're going ahead with an arrest?"

"Detectives Chambers and Drake took him into custody yesterday evening."

Luna and I shared a look. That explained the early morning visitor that was causing my floors to be refinished.

"So why am I here now?"

"First, because we want you to go over your statement with an F.B.I. agent to ensure it's as ironclad as it can be. And second, because I wanted you to see how serious we are about bringing Vale to justice. We are prepared to put the entire might of our combined agencies behind you, Ms. Massey."

"I've already said I'll testify."

Laurent sighed. "Yes, and I appreciate that, but with a criminal as high profile as Vale, more often than not, witnesses recant or disappear. I'd like your assurances you won't back out. I'd also like to put you in police custody to guard against the second outcome."

"I'm not going to recant or withdraw my statement, Mr. Laurent, and as for disappearing… I guarantee you, I'm well protected. There is zero chance someone will get to me."

He put his hands on his ample hips and stared at the floor before pinning me with his eyes. "You're refusing police protection?"

"Yes, and I will continue to do so."

He nodded, but he wasn't happy. "In that case, I want to know where you are at all times."

"I'm afraid you can't."

He whipped around, and I backed up a step—bumping into Luna.

"That's non-negotiable, Ms. Massey. I want to know you're safe, and I can't do that if I don't know where you are."

I straightened my spine. "Mr. Laurent, unless you plan to kidnap or arrest me, I will not be sharing my location. You can know where I am when I am standing in front of you—and that's it."

He looked at someone over my shoulder before relenting, then pointed me toward the agent who would go over my statement with me, and stormed off like a toddler. A large, balding toddler with hairy arms. The visual made me chuckle, which got me a weird look from Luna. "Ask me in the car," I whispered.

It took an hour and a half for the agent to be satisfied with my recounting of events and the answers to his questions. I was tired, cranky, and my cooter was sore. All I wanted was to get home and pour half a bag of Epsom salts into the tub and soak until the water was cold.

But the day wasn't done with me yet.

THIRTY-FOUR

JADE IS FINE. The refrain was on repeat in my head until it was replaced with: *Jade is fine, but the last time she was out of your sight, she was attacked and injured.*

I stood up with enough force to send my chair into the wall behind me. All conversation stopped and everyone looked at me.

"Sorry, I need to move."

The rooms on the bottom floor of Roul's house flowed one into the next and formed a circle around a central staircase to the upstairs. It was an excellent pacing track.

"What does your bond tell you?" Drym called as I passed through the living room.

I focused on the dancing lights as I made a lap. "That she's fine," I answered as I passed him.

I saw Kendal shake her head before entering the kitchen.

"If it were me…," she said.

Drym grunted. "I'd be going crazy too."

"Exactly. Leave him be, Drym."

On my fourth lap, Nanna blocked my path. When I moved to go around her, she moved with me.

"That's enough. You're making me dizzy. Just call her, for fuck's sake."

My jaw dropped open. Using the phone had never entered my mind. I scattered the group of cell phones on the kitchen counter, digging to find mine.

Quin shouted, "Hey!" at my rough treatment of the electronics, but they were all in near indestructible cases—a necessity for us, since we didn't want to replace them every time we made a phone call.

I mashed the phone button and then Jade's name. It rang once and then went straight to voice mail. Her cheerful tone told me to leave a message, and she'd call me right back. After the beep, I took too long thinking of what to say, and a robotic voice asked me if I was happy with the message.

I tried again, and this time managed, "Wanted to make sure you're okay," before hanging up.

I clenched the phone, staring at the screen like it might magically light up with Jade's name. The bond told me she was safe, but her not answering left a gnawing feeling in my gut. Behind me, there was a clatter—Nanna dropped her tea mug in the sink with a sharp thud.

"I'm sure she's just busy," Kendal ventured, her voice soft but not entirely convincing. "It's only been a few minutes."

"Busy?" I scraped my claws across the back of my neck. "Yes, maybe. Or maybe… Maybe I'm just being paranoid," I added, a little too loud, hoping to convince myself.

Drym pushed off the couch and came into the kitchen, arms crossed over his broad chest. "You don't need to explain anything to us. But this pacing in circles is getting on everyone's nerves—including yours."

I couldn't argue with that. My pulse throbbed in my ears, the same refrain beating like a drum: Jade is fine. Jade is fine. Except… the last time I assumed she was fine, she ended up hurt. I growled in frustration. I couldn't follow her. It was still daylight. I was trapped in the compound until dark.

I stared at the red motes of light that bobbed around me, willing myself to calm down.

A small hand tapped my forearm, and I looked down to find River standing in front of me.

"I know where they are. I'll go."

I shook my head. It still wouldn't be me.

She held up her phone and then grabbed mine, dialing herself. "I'll leave it on speaker. You'll be able to hear everything."

I nodded. "Yes. Please."

As she stepped through the door I called after her. "Thank you."

She stopped and looked over her shoulder. "We take care of our own, Thurl."

In that moment, I finally felt like a creature that others cared about and would help. My entire life it had been just me and my brothers. It was hard to rely on someone else. Hard to trust. She still scared me, but I trusted Zeus. He trusted River.

I hoped she would find nothing, and my brothers could laugh at how silly I'd been. I hoped to hear her voice chiding me for sending River after her on the other end of the line.

I would let them tease as much as they wanted if it were true. I couldn't lose Jade. Without her sugar and sunshine, I would be a dark shell. To have the depth of the mate bond ripped away—it would be too much to bear.

I sank into a crouch, the phone still cradled in my hands as I listened to the sounds of River getting into her vehicle and driving.

Please, please let her be okay.

THIRTY-FIVE

I HAD THE worst headache I'd ever had. I needed to take some medicine and find a dark room to curl up in. I wondered if Thurl had aspirin. Probably not. I can't imagine the wyrfangs got headaches. He said they couldn't get sick. I was thinking about the flu but that probably meant headaches, too.

I rolled over to ask him if he had a first aid kit and my arm scraped along the floor.

Wait. Why was I on the floor? Why was the floor rough like badly poured concrete?

I pushed myself up and cracked open an eye.

The floor *was* badly poured, rough concrete and I was not in Thurl's house. I wasn't in the joint task force warehouse, either. I had no idea where I was.

A thick layer of dust didn't help cushion the floor, but it let me see a few sets of footprints leading to a door on the far wall. Mold covered the ceiling and had made it about halfway down one wall. There was a dirty window with a pane missing over a cracked sink, but I could see the bars on the outside from where I sat.

"Luna?" My brain punished me with a sharp stab when I turned to look for her. I was alone.

I closed my eyes and took a few calming breaths. Panicking would do me no good and just make my head hurt worse.

The arm propping me up sported a line of blood running from my inner elbow to my wrist. The hole looked like the kind you got from an IV. Despite my best efforts, anxiety surged.

Someone had injected me with something?

I struggled to remember what happened, but after stepping out of the warehouse and walking toward the SUV, everything was a dark blur.

I pushed at the wound and hissed. The red lights I'd grown used to enough to have forgotten about flared bright.

Oh no.

Thurl would be going crazy.

Judging by what made it past the grime on the window, it was still daylight.

The door opened, and light rushed in, blinding me.

"Oh good, you're awake."

Rough hands yanked me to my feet, and I stumbled as the man pulled me along. I blinked and swallowed down a wave of nausea. "What did you give me?"

"A sedative. I needed you easy to handle."

I looked over and forced my eyes to focus on his face.

"Officer Phillips?"

"You remember me?"

I nodded and then regretted it. "Yep."

He sighed. "Too bad."

I didn't ask what that meant. After a short hallway, we entered a living room that was only marginally in better shape than the room I'd been in. A table stretched along one wall, currently occupied by a man's body. A woman in scrubs stood next to it, arguing with another man whose back was to me.

"You can't expect me to save him when he's full of this many holes!"

"I can, and I do."

The front door opened and a third man who rivaled the breadth of Zeus walked in. A towering figure, standing well over six feet, who seemed built entirely of muscle. His tight black t-shirt exposed gray scale tattoos covering both arms, marred by scars that crisscrossed his knuckles and forearms, evidence of countless brawls.

His face would be handsome if he wasn't wearing a scowl. He was a stark contrast to Vale's elegance.

Then I saw a tiny figure behind him.

A little girl I instantly recognized.

"Sophia?"

The nurse spun toward the door and Sophia's eyes went impossibly wide as she took in the scene. The other woman lunged for her, but the businessman grabbed her arm and yanked her back.

"She's fine, and will remain that way as long as you stay focused on your task."

My head throbbed, my elbow stung and I was so confused I wanted to cry. "What is going on? Where's Luna?"

The businessman turned around slowly and I gaped at Adrian Vale.

He tilted his head at me and then pinned Officer Phillips with a death stare.

"Why is she here?"

"You told me to grab her, boss."

He backed up a step, and since he hadn't let go of my arm, I did too.

His tone was deadly quiet when he said, "I told you to grab her, not bring her here. So I'll ask one more time. Why is she here?"

Phillips audibly swallowed. "I… I… I…" He stammered the word without adding any others.

Vale slashed his hand through the air. "It's done." He directed his next words to Sophia. "Sit down, sweetheart, and watch mommy work. Everything's fine."

She looked from him to her mother and back again. Then she made her way at a snail's speed to the couch and sat, avoiding the rips and springs that poked through.

I swung my focus to the nurse and finally recognized her from parent-teacher meetings. "Mrs. Calder?"

Her lips pinched shut as Vale spoke.

"Ms. Massey, please don't distract her."

"Where is Luna?" My head was full of cobwebs, but I'd managed to knock a few down.

"I don't know anyone by that name."

Phillips found his voice. "Her bodyguard."

"Ah. In that case, answer the lady Phillips."

"She was a problem. I shot her."

I jerked in his grasp. Tears sprang to my eyes and I blinked furiously. I refused to cry in front of these assholes.

Vale scrubbed his hand down his face. "Do you not have a single brain cell, Phillips?" He didn't let him answer. "Shut up. Not another word."

"I don't understand. Why am I here and not dead?" I couldn't figure out why he didn't just shoot me, too.

"I was hoping we could come to a mutually beneficial agreement."

"How on earth could I benefit you?"

He smiled and it was the definition of slimy.

"You have managed to elude me and all of my associates, thus, you have skill at hiding that supersedes those in my employ's ability to find what they're looking for. It would prove useful to have a skill like that at my disposal."

I glanced at Mrs. Calder, who was throwing bloody stacks of gauze on the floor and poking inside the man on the table's body.

"That's … not a skill I can transfer to anyone else."

He steepled his fingers at his chin. "Are you unable or unwilling to teach someone else?"

"Unable." I yanked at Phillps's hold again and managed to get free this time. I didn't move my feet. There was no point. I wouldn't outrun Phillips or Wall of Muscle, much less a bullet.

"That's disappointing. I thought you were a teacher."

"It's not a lack of skill, Mr. Vale, that prevents me. It's the simple fact that my solution only worked because of who I am. No one else could take advantage of it."

He dropped his hands and cocked his head. "Interesting. Explain."

"No."

I saw the change in his demeanor. He went from behaving like he was at a business dinner to pure rage in the blink of an eye. "No?"

I nodded.

"Do you know how I got to be so powerful, Ms. Massey?"

"I do not."

He moved to the couch and picked up a lock of Sophia's hair, letting it run through his fingers. "I find out what people want, or what they can't live without, and then I exploit it."

He looked back at me. "I'll figure out your pressure point, eventually. It will be a lot easier on both of us if you simply tell me now instead of making me go to the trouble."

"I'm sure your minions won't mind doing the research." I stopped. "Why did you murder that boy?"

His face shuttered. "He stole from me."

"No, why did *you* do it? Why not have Wall of Muscle or another lackey do it?" I waved in the wall's direction.

"I gained power by leveraging my skill at ferreting out information, but that often isn't enough to keep it. I killed that boy because it's good to remind everyone what lengths I'm willing to go, what I'm capable of doing, to stay at the top."

He didn't get to continue his villain speech because Mrs. Calder started slamming her fist against the bloody man's chest, punctuating each hit with a yelled, "Fuck!"

THIRTY-SIX

I HEARD A car door open, then close, then running on gravel.

"Shit, shit, shit. Call Zeus. Tell him to get the cavalry to my location."

I growled. "I'm not hanging up."

"There's like thirty cell phones on the kitchen counter," she yelled, "use one of them!"

Nanna grabbed the one at the top of the stack and held it up. "Whose is this?" Quin raised his hand and Nanna tossed it to him. "Do what she says!"

I strained to hear what was happening over the roar in my ears.

"Luna! Stay with me! We're only on episode six of *Burning Desire* and I am not watching the rest without you!"

Luna's weak voice answered her. "My snark is too good."

"Damn right it is."

I heard Quin talking to Zeus, heard Zeus shouting and then everything went quiet until the crunch of tires and doors opening came from the phone I held too tight.

Zeus's strained voice called out, "River!"

"It's not me, it's Luna. Where's Ghost?"

"Ten seconds out."

"Where is Jade?" My roar hung in the air.

"We'll find her," Zeus answered.

"She's not there? Where is the district attorney?"

"The building is locked. There's no one else here."

Air sawed in and out of my lungs. Roul entered my vision, a wall blocking me from running into the daylight and through human streets.

"It will be dark in twenty minutes."

I flexed my shoulders and dropped the phone. "Too long! In twenty minutes she could be..." I couldn't bring myself to say it. My heart felt like it would leave my body, my chest caved in and my throat closed.

"Not going to happen, brother."

Roul's steady voice calmed me, and Drym helped further.

"You would feel if she was hurt."

I nodded and scanned my body for the minutest twinge of pain. The inside of my elbow stung, but aside from that, she seemed whole.

I focused when Kragen started strategizing. Every second that ticked by was an eternity, but when Roul finally said, "Let's go," we were ready.

Hold on, kitten. I will tear the world apart to find you.

THIRTY-SEVEN

I TRACKED THE sun through the small window in the front door as it set. Vale allowed me to sit on the couch, and I held Sophia's hand as we both watched her mother try to save a dead man.

Vale didn't pace or fidget. He looked like he was at a business dinner, ready to make a high-powered deal.

I wanted to vomit.

Officer Phillips had left without a backward glance, but from the look Vale gave Wall of Muscle, I suspected he wasn't long for this world.

Every few minutes, Vale tried to get a rise out of me, gaging my reaction as he asked about different aspects of my life. I knew he was probing for weaknesses, and I kept my face as neutral as possible as I answered the innocuous questions and ignored some randomly to throw him off.

I knew Thurl would come. Our bond danced out the door like a hiker who'd just run face first into a spiderweb. I tried to send calming vibes down the tether, but I didn't think it worked that way.

I looked up at the slab of beef in front of me. "What's your name?"

He just grunted.

Vale's curiosity was piqued. "Why do you want to know?"

I snorted. "Because I'm tired of calling him Wall of Muscle in my head."

Vale laughed. Even that was a controlled, calculated sound. He nodded and waved his hand at the man.

"Briggs." He didn't look like he was hungover, but his voice sure sounded like he'd been drinking rotgut since he was five.

The politeness ingrained in me since birth kicked in. "Nice to meet you, Briggs."

The corner of his mouth quirked. I figured that was the most emotion a giant rock was capable of.

Tension ratcheted to an impossible level as Mrs. Calder failed to create a zombie.

She screamed in frustration, and her hands dropped limp to her sides. "He's past saving, Mr. Vale."

Adrian got closer to the table than I expected, but he didn't seem to have a problem getting his clothes or hands bloody. He poked at the corpse and sighed with a click of his tongue. "I'm disappointed, Mrs. Calder."

"Please don't hurt her."

The tremble in her voice made my heart ache. Sophia stiffened next to me, her fingers tightening around mine.

Briggs didn't move, but his hands flexed at his sides, the faintest shift of tension rolling across his boulder-like shoulders. I stared up at him in horror but found him looking at Vale instead. Weird.

A wolf's howl sent chills down my spine. A slow grin spread across my lips. Darkness had fallen.

"What the fuck was that?"

It was the first time I'd seen Vale's composure crack. He looked at Briggs, who shrugged. With his bodyguard unconcerned, the mask fell back into place. He sighed dramatically.

"My compatriot is dead. There is no longer a reason to stay here." He turned to me. "Miss Massey, would you like to reconsider your position?"

The smile on my lips made his eyes widen ever so slightly.

"I've already explained why I can't."

His eyes flicked from me to Sophia and then to our clasped hands. "Not even to save the girl?"

Sophia's mother whimpered.

"You wouldn't," I snarled.

His laugh was bitter. "You have no idea what I would or wouldn't do."

I looked at Briggs, ready to plead, and caught a damn near imperceptible shake of his head. I straightened my spine and stood, putting Sophia behind me. "The depth of your depravity makes no difference in this case, but I will fight tooth and nail before I let you hurt a single hair on her head."

Mrs. Calder's hand covered her mouth as silent tears tracked down her cheeks.

"Very brave, Miss Massey, but neither your teeth nor nails are any match against Briggs."

"Maybe not, but I'll do my best to damage you before he gets to me." The tiny motes of light shivered around me and another howl rang from outside, closer this time.

Thurl was coming, and I couldn't stop my grin.

Vale strode to the door and craned his neck to see as much of the outside as possible through the dirty window in the door.

I mouthed, "It's going to be all right," to Mrs. Calder, but judging by her shell-shocked expression, she wasn't processing anything around her.

Adrian stepped back from the door, his movements controlled, but I could see the tension coiling in his shoulders. The second howl had rattled him, even if he tried to hide it.

"Briggs," he said sharply, "go check it out."

Briggs hesitated. It was brief—a fraction of a second—but I caught it. He turned toward the door, his steps heavy, the floor creaking like it would give up at any moment.

"I wouldn't," I said, my voice steady.

Briggs paused mid-step, his bulk casting a shadow across the room. He glanced at me, the faintest flicker of curiosity—or doubt—crossing his face. Vale turned slowly, his eyes narrowing.

"And why is that, Miss Massey?"

I shrugged and kept my tone neutral. "Just saying it might not be a good idea to wander outside without knowing what's out there."

Vale's lips curved into a thin, humorless smile. "How thoughtful of you to care about Briggs' well-being."

"More like my own," I stated with false concern. "Having him here makes me a smaller target."

Vale's smile didn't falter, but his eyes darkened, sharp with calculation. He gestured toward the door again. "Check it."

A tic appeared in Briggs's jaw. A few tense seconds passed before he gave a curt nod, but when he opened the door, another man shouldered his way inside.

"Boss, something's out there."

"What?"

The man shook, an all over body tremble. His eyes darted around the room like he needed to escape—or a place to hide. "Didn't get a look at it, but it took out Brick and Niko."

A growl shattered the silence that followed, low, close, and angry.

Vale's composure faltered. His fingers twitched as his gaze flicked toward the door. Vale turned back to me, his mask back in place. His movements were too smooth, too rehearsed, as he approached. "Do you know what I find fascinating, Miss Massey?" he asked, his tone light but edged with menace. "You don't seem alarmed."

I crossed my arms over my chest. "I have a good poker face. Believe me, I'm scared." I added a dramatic shiver to my performance.

His laugh was sharp, almost amused, but his eyes remained cold. "You're no actress. Do you know what's out there?"

Behind him, Briggs' attention shifted subtly, his gaze darting toward the door. A faint growl, barely audible but unmistakable, rumbled outside. My pulse quickened. Thurl was closer than anyone here realized.

Briggs shifted, moving his hulk in front of both me and Sophia.

I gripped the little girl's hand tighter and let my lips curve into a slow, deliberate smile. Vale's eyes narrowed.

"I told you my hiding place wouldn't work for anyone but me," I said, the tether to Thurl thrumming with quiet determination. "And I'm really looking forward to watching you see why."

THIRTY-EIGHT

THE NEIGHBORHOOD WAS dark, most of the houses long abandoned and clinging desperately to their foundations. Vale had made this almost too easy.

Three thugs patrolled the target house. They were unorganized and sloppy. Amateurs.

Roul took one out without even getting dirty. I grabbed the other as he came around the corner, his eyes going wide as I slashed my claws across his throat.

The third was smarter. As soon as his buddies went quiet, he ran for the front door. I could hear voices from the front room and clocked each one. The thug, a man with too-smooth a voice, and Jade.

I flexed my claws. She sounded unhurt, but until I could see her, see for myself she was okay, I'd remain on edge.

I stalked closer to the door, Kragen at my back. Roul was on the opposite side with Drym. Quin and Cavi covered the back, in case any of them decided to run.

Kragen decided a direct approach was best. These human criminals wouldn't expect us, and with so few being present, it would be a walk in the park. Instead of busting the door down, he planned a stealthier entry, to keep our advantage as long as possible.

We were tough, not bulletproof.

Roul reached out and slowly turned the doorknob. A quarter into the rotation, a click sounded. I almost missed it, straining to make out Jade's words.

"Down!"

The four of us hit the ground as the concrete walk in front of the door exploded. Concrete and shrapnel buried into my shoulder and back. Rage, hot and swift, filled my body. My vision blurred, red bleeding over everything. My mind narrowed to a single point—a single objective.

Jade.

I was up and through the door before the dust settled.

The thug from outside was the first to go. His scream turned into a gurgle as I tore out his throat. Movement swung my head to the left, where another man backed himself into a corner. That was a mistake. I was on him in two strides, my head cleared enough to clock the fancy suit he wore.

This was Vale then.

His mouth opened and closed but no sound emerged. I dug my claws into his chest and yanked. He fell to the side, and I dropped the chunk of skin, bone, muscle and organs I'd ripped from him.

A third threat stood between me and Jade. Jade was trying to get around him, to come to me, but he kept pushing her back.

Here was more of a challenge. I stalked the big man, sizing up his skill as he dropped into a fighting stance. My brothers crowded into the room but a pointed look at Kragen had him holding them back.

Jade was saying something, but the roar in my ears was still too loud.

I watched her jostle for position with the man until she brought her heel down on his foot… hard. He threw his hands up in surrender and backed off. The unexpected move gave me enough pause for the fog to clear. Sound rushed in.

"Stop, Thurl! He's with us!"

I blinked and studied the man again. With a flick of his head, his eyes went from human brown to otherworldly gold. The pupils narrowed to a point and a rolling chuff came from his chest.

I relaxed, but didn't turn my focus from him. He was definitely Society, but why was he here? Why would he be with a human criminal?

"Jade." My voice was little more than a rumble. I held out my hand—the clean one—and she rushed into my hold. With my brothers at my back to watch the unknown supernatural, I buried my nose in her hair and inhaled.

"I'm okay. It's okay. It's over."

I didn't know if she was telling me or herself. "You're not injured?"

She shook her head. "No. It was Officer Phillips. He injected me with some kind of sedative." Tears sprang in her eyes. "He said Luna was… that he'd shot her and she was…"

"Zeus says she'll be fine."

She pulled back and looked up at me, so I nodded to reassure her. I watched her face crumple before she buried it in my chest, her shoulders heaving with racking sobs.

"Shh, kitten. You're okay now. I've got you."

I studied the other creature and then noticed the little girl and another woman. The woman had the girl wrapped in her arms while the creature spoke to them softly.

"Who are you?"

Before I could take Jade home, I needed to ascertain if he was a threat. A threat would not be allowed to leave intact.

"Briggs Stone. I'm a Society Operative. I've been undercover with Silver Fang for two years." He stared at Vale's corpse and sighed. "We wanted him alive, but I can see there wasn't a snowball's chance in hell of that happening."

"Why would you want the head of a criminal organization alive?"

I didn't care, but Kragen was ever strategic. The more information, the better, in his opinion.

"The power vacuum left when The Level lost its leadership made the entire region volatile. We'd hoped to avoid a repeat situation." He smiled, showing off canines just a little too sharp, a little too long to be human. "And he was easy to control."

He tilted his head at us. "What are you?"

Kragen started talking and I didn't bother sticking around. Halfway out the door, Jade called over my shoulder, "What about Sophia and Mrs. Calder?"

"They'll get home safe, I'll ensure it."

I still didn't trust Briggs, but the relief in Jade's eyes made me reevaluate my opinion of him.

I took her home and settled her on the couch with Sir Purrs-a-lot while I washed off the gore that clung to my forearm. Nanna wrapped her in a blanket and fussed over her until I was done. I scooped her into my arms and held her on my lap while I breathed and satisfied myself she was okay.

After all five of my brothers checked on her (and me), and she'd finished a large mug of hot chocolate with whipped cream, she fell asleep in my arms. I took her to our bed, away from other eyes, and tucked her close to my chest.

"Sleep, kitten."

EPILOGUE

IF THURL COULD share spleens with me, he would. I knew it would be a while before he let me out of his sight again, but it was getting ridiculous. I couldn't go to the bathroom without leaving the door open. Showering alone was a thing of the past.

You'd think I would be used to that, since the cats never let me pee in peace either, but it's different when you're talking about a seven-foot-tall monster.

"I think I'll be okay in the living room by myself, Thurl."

His ears drooped, but I stood my ground. The constant hovering chafed.

"Officer Phillips—"

"Would be an idiot to step foot inside the compound and would be dead before he got to the common."

He looked around the living room as if he worried the man hid under the couch.

"Seriously, Thurl. I'm going to get cranky if you don't give me some space."

He finally retreated into the kitchen with Nanna, who hadn't been much better than him, but at least she smothered me with food instead of literally smothering me.

I'd moved in with him days after my ordeal with Vale. Neither of us wanted to be apart. We'd melded our households seamlessly and my house was going on the market in a week. I'd taken a leave of absence from teaching. I wasn't sure I'd go back. I wasn't sure what I'd do at that point, but I didn't want to be where Thurl couldn't go for most of the day. We'd figure something out. In the meantime, I would let him take care of me. Turns out, the nest egg Society had given each of the 'fangs was more than enough to sustain me, him, and my dozen cats for life.

Nanna visited every week. She said it was to check on me, but I think it was more because she got a massive ego boost from the 'fangs enthusiastic enjoyment of her food. And Roul, who remained her favorite to fuss over.

There was a debate raging between the 'fangs, Supe Sec, and the Society council over how to handle Officer Phillips. At that point, I didn't care. There was no way he'd get to me again, and if he tried, he'd take himself out of the council's protection. He didn't have a clue that's all that was keeping him alive.

I scooched into the corner of our plush leather sectional and stretched my legs out. Pawssonova was the first to claim his spot on my lap, leaving Whisker to assume the role as bookend to my left thigh and Catticus Finch on the right. Cameow curled up on my shins. I'd be screaming to move after about twenty minutes, but for now, I sank back and enjoyed the warmth.

I woke up my Kindle and queued the latest book club read. Not two pages in, someone knocked on the door.

"Are we expecting company?" I asked Nanna as she shuffled past to answer it.

She just shrugged.

The cacophony that erupted when she opened the door sent the four cats who'd been happily dozing on me, plus another few stationed in various places around the room, skittering across the floor and into hiding places.

"The cavalry has arrived!"

I craned my neck over the back of the sofa and watched as people spilled into the house, clown car style. River carried the largest bowl of popcorn I'd ever laid eyes on. Luna, fully recovered, but with the smallest scar she showed off like a trophy, followed her.

"More like the marshmallow army," Kendal said as she made her way in.

River nodded. "Yep! I marshmallow'd the troops!" She cackled with delight at her own joke.

Two more women followed Kendal. One of them practically vibrated with excitement as she made a beeline for me. She shoved a wad of fabric at me, her eyes sparkling.

"Hi! I'm Virginia! Welcome to the SMC. Here's your official shirt."

Her grin was ear to ear and infectious. I shook the fabric into a jersey. "Thank you, I love it."

She nodded like that was a forgone conclusion. I supposed to her, it was.

River was behind Thurl, pushing him to the door and yelling, "Shoo!" at him. "This is girls only! Go to Roul's."

She was surprisingly strong for being so little. If I tried that, I would just push myself across the floor. She was actually making headway. Not much, but he was moving.

I laughed. "Go on. I'll be fine."

He twisted and contorted his neck to keep his eyes on me until the last possible second, when River shut the door. Around me the others were getting comfortable, finding space on the sectional or the floor. The other woman I hadn't met yet held out her hand.

"I'm Gaelynn."

"It's nice to meet you," I said automatically as we shook.

She laughed. "It's overwhelming but you'll learn that when Virginia gets an idea, it's best just to roll with it."

When everyone was snug in what I could tell would be their designated spots in my house, River turned on the television and started a Seductflix movie. Wolf whistles and catcalls ensued as soon as the hero entered the frame.

He was handsome enough, but he wasn't a monster.

Luna bumped my shoulder like she'd read my thoughts. "They're adapting a paranormal romance next. We'll be back to watch the first episode as soon as it's out." She paused. "I hope you don't mind. You have the biggest couch. And Nanna."

I laughed. "I don't mind."

She grinned and for the next few hours I laughed so hard my sides hurt while the ladies joked and snarked about the movie.

A month ago, I would have told you to get professional help if you'd said I'd witness a murder, much less be bonded to a beast with horns and claws who made my heart (and, let's face it, my pussy) sigh with contentment. As I sat there, surrounded by women fast becoming friends, I thanked the universe I was wearing my glasses that night.

GIVE MOUSE A TREAT

Mouse would be very pleased if you'd leave a review and let us know what you thought. It doesn't have to be long or elaborate, just a few words or a sentence would mean the world to us. (He gets a special treat every time I get a review.)

(That's not the only time he gets treats.
I'm not a monster.)

amazon
Write a customer review

+review on goodreads

BookBub
Review

THANK YOU

Thank you for reading Guarded by a Monster! I sincerely hope you enjoyed Thurl and Jade's story.

Subscribe to my newsletter for updates and snippets, plus other bonus goodies: https://kenziekelly.com/subscribe

If you just want to know when I have a new release, follow me on Amazon and they'll email you when a new book is available.

This book was professionally edited and proofread, but typos are like rabbits, they multiply when you aren't looking. If you find one, please copy it and the sentence so I can find it and email me at herself@kenziekelly.com.

ABOUT THE AUTHOR

Kenzie grew up in Bluff Park, a suburb of Birmingham, AL in a very improper Southern household. She now lives in a suburb Northeast of Atlanta, GA. She married her college sweetheart and has two sons. She is adored by a Pit Bull and tolerated by two cats. She drinks far too much Diet Coke and feels like she can tackle anything as long as she has a book showing her how.

Though other interests have come and gone, four obsessions have remained constant: horses, photography, reading, and writing.

Her job as chief child wrangler and household CEO consumed most of her energy (creative and otherwise) until April 2017 when the characters in her head demanded their stories be told. She's been writing ever since.

Also by Kenzie:

The Ka'atari Warriors Series (Sci-Fi Romance)
The Superhuman Security Series (Paranormal Romance)
The Whiskey Vex Series (Urban Fantasy)
The Empyrean Series (Romantic Fantasy)

For a full, up-to-date list of books, visit her website:
https://kenziekelly.com.

Made in United States
Cleveland, OH
01 October 2025

20999844R00173

1